THE INFAMOUS
Frankie Lorde

STEALING GREENWICH

CHECK OUT ALL OF FRANKIE'S "MARKS"

Next up
Book 2: **GOING WILD**

THE INFAMOUS
Frankie Lorde

STEALING
GREENWICH

BRITTANY GERAGOTELIS

PIXEL✚INK

PIXEL✚INK

Pixel+Ink is a division of TGM Development Corp.

Printed and bound in August 2020 at Maple Press, York, PA, U.S.A.

Cover and interior design by Steve Scott

www.pixelandinkbooks.com

Library of Congress Control Number: 2020938107

HC ISBN 978-1-64595-026-4

eBook ISBN 978-1-64595-043-1

First Edition

1 3 5 7 9 10 8 6 4 2

To my boys.
In life, it's okay to be Robin Hood
and not the king.

THE INFAMOUS
Frankie Lorde

STEALING
GREENWICH

Entry One

People say writing in journals can be therapeutic. Well, at least that's what my therapist says. I just think it's an easy way for other people to find out all your secrets.

And seriously, who wants that?

But alas, my therapist, Dr. Janine Deerchuck—yep, that's really her name—thinks it would be "beneficial" to me if I kept one, so here we are.

She's suggested that I use this journal to write down all my hopes, and dreams, and fears, and blah, blah, blah . . . I figure if I'm going to do this, I'll use it as a record of every awesome thing I've ever done. And when I'm finished filling up every last lined page in this black-and-white notebook, I'll send it to my dad to let him know what I've been up to since he went away.

And that's what brings us to Dr. Deerchuck and this journal in the first place:

Dear old Dad.

Don't get me wrong, my dad is *awesome*. He's one of the smartest, coolest, greatest dads on the planet. He's practically raised me all on his own, and has taken me to places that other kids don't even know exist—like Tanzania and Cat Island. He lets me stay up late, his favorite food

1

is pancakes, and he doesn't even care if I occasionally sneak-watch *Game of Thrones*.

He should be in the Hall of Fame of dads, right?

In reality? Not so much.

But he *is* famous. Just not for his mad dad skills.

Let me draw you a picture of my life with Dad. This is what happened during our last daddy/daughter outing:

Dad and I were in Paris, hanging out at a hip local spot, drinking *café crèmes*—a fancy term for milky coffee, in case you didn't know—and people-watching. It's one of our favorite things to do. We take turns coming up with backgrounds and stories for strangers who walk by.

Trust me, it's a lot more entertaining than it sounds.

I'd just dug into the most delicious chocolate croissant when Dad discreetly pointed to a lady crossing the street. She was wearing a smart-looking trench coat and sporting a short, boyish haircut.

"So, Frankie, what's her deal?" Dad asked me.

I studied her like she was a work of art, noting her appearance and the way she moved and then taking in any other details she was giving away. If you know what to look for, it's easy to tell exactly who a person is within the first fifteen seconds of meeting them.

And who taught me this cool superpower? My dad.

See, I told you he's awesome.

"She's American. That's obvious. Look at her shoes," I said, gesturing at the boringly practical black flats the woman was wearing. "She's trying to act like she's not in a rush, but she is. And she's nervous about something. Maybe she's meeting someone for the first time? Her trench coat isn't a fashion statement. It's there to hide what's underneath, which appears to be . . ."

I squinted in the midmorning sun in an attempt to see better.

" . . . very unstylish and poorly fitting pants," I finished. "She's a professional of some kind, though her appearance doesn't seem to be a concern of hers, so I'd guess she's not in media or entertainment, or any field where she has to sell things to people, for that matter."

The woman's eyes flitted from side to side furtively as if she was looking for someone. And that's when it happened.

Her gaze fell on me and we locked eyes.

It was only for a few seconds, but there was a recognition there that I could see right away. Almost immediately, she was lifting her hand up to her ear, and I watched as her lips moved soundlessly.

"She's a cop," I said bluntly, realizing I should've figured it out earlier. My dad probably had her pegged when he first picked her out of the crowd. He'd just been testing me.

And I'd failed.

"Dad—" I started.

"Play it cool, Frankie," my dad said calmly as he picked up his still-steaming *café crème* and took a long sip.

"What's the plan?" I asked almost immediately, having played out this scenario a million times in my head.

3

I looked around the square to try to suss out all possible escape routes. Within a few seconds I already knew of five different ways we could get out of there before the trench coat lady even reached us.

"I'll spill my drink, you go inside to get napkins," I said, thinking out loud. "Head out the back and down the alley and I'll meet you at our rendezvous point—"

"It's over, Frankie," my dad said, smiling at me.

"It's not," I said, confused. "She won't even get here for another ten seconds."

"She's the last one to the party," Dad said, gesturing over his shoulder to the table directly behind us. "There's nothing to do."

I swiveled my gaze without moving my head and immediately saw what he was talking about. Two serious-looking guys in suits sat at a tiny round table nearby, staring straight at us. Cups of coffee sat in front of them, but there was no steam, which meant the coffee had long since gone cold. Or possibly, there hadn't been anything in there to begin with.

Another detail I'd missed earlier. Man, I was off my game.

But Dad wasn't. Per usual, he knew everything that was going on around him.

And now he was telling me the jig was up.

"But, Dad," I argued, my voice coming out all squeaky and high like I hated. "You said there's always a plan B."

"There is," he answered, patting my hand reassuringly. "We're just not using it *today*."

An arm reached in between us then and I looked up to see one of the men from the next table helping Dad to his feet and pulling his arms behind his back.

Trench Coat Lady finally reached us, slightly out of breath from her walk but prickling with excitement.

"Tom Lorde, you're under arrest for fraud, forgery, swindling, grand larceny . . . ," she began as she listed off all his offenses from memory. I wondered how long she'd been practicing the speech. Hours? Days? Years?

And without another word to me, she swept Dad away and into a waiting car.

Entry Two

So, yeah. My dad's sort of a thief.

Well, not just *any* thief. I believe after his arrest and subsequent trial, the papers called him "the most infamous international thief in modern history." Which, of course, made me roll my eyes, but I was also secretly a little proud. I knew Dad was good. I just hadn't realized he was *infamous* good.

After that day, my life turned completely upside down. This is the reason I have to see Dr. Deerchuck and write in this stupid journal.

Make more sense now?

Anyway, the journal is kind of the least of my worries currently. Because now that my dad is living out his infamy in a prison in Virginia and the law says I have to have an adult watching my every move, I'm being sent to live with my uncle Scotty.

Uncle Scotty is my dad's brother. He's younger than my dad by, well, a lot, and I haven't seen him in more than five years. Since before Dad decided to take our show on the road and travel the world.

I don't remember a lot about him, but from what I *do* recall, he's not all that bad. Whenever we visited, he'd always order pizza or Chinese takeout for dinner and tell me embarrassing stories about my dad when he was a kid.

And my dad liked Uncle Scotty, too. Once he confessed that as far as younger brothers went, Uncle Scotty wasn't all that annoying. And for someone like my dad, who didn't actually like all that many people—and trusted even fewer—that was high praise.

But as cool as Uncle Scotty may be, there's still one big, glaring, red-alert problem with going to live with him.

He's a cop.

And as you can probably guess . . . thieves and cops don't exactly mix.

Entry Three

So you can see my dilemma, right?

Recently caught thief going to live with the right hand of the law? The whole situation could practically be a Shakespearean play. In fact, I'm not entirely sure it isn't. Dad and I only made it through half of Willy's work before my studies were cut short by the FBI.

What I'm trying to say is that me going to live with my cop uncle is definitely a recipe for disaster.

Not everyone agrees with me, though.

"I really think this will be good for you, Frankie," Dr. Deerchuck said as we sat on the commuter train headed north.

I'd been in New York City the past week, participating in daily mandatory intensive therapy with Dr. Deerchuck, meant to prepare me for my new life with Uncle Scotty.

But how were you supposed to prepare for something like that?

Well, apparently it involved a *lot* of talking. And then more talking. And yep, more talking.

Now all I wanted to do on our trip up to Connecticut was *not* talk.

Dr. Deerchuck, however, hadn't stopped talking since we'd sat down.

"Frankie? Are you listening to me?" she asked, forcing her face in front of mine so I'd have to make eye contact with her. "I *do* think this will be good for you."

"I'm glad you think so," I said under my breath as I evaded her gaze, looking around the rest of the train car instead.

"What was that?" Dr. Deerchuck asked, not quite hearing what I'd said.

I forced myself to brighten. "I said, 'I should think so.'"

Dr. Deerchuck beamed, seeming happy to have gotten through to another one of her patients.

"Now, I understand you and your uncle haven't seen each other in quite some time, so things might not click into place right away," she continued. "But I promise, if you just keep an open mind and are willing to adapt to your new situation, things will get back to normal in no time."

I nodded as I looked out the window at the buildings and houses we were zipping by. I knew this was what she wanted from me and the sooner I complied, the sooner the torture would be over.

"And of course, if anything comes up, you always have this. . . . ," she said, handing over my journal.

I frowned as I saw the familiar black-and-white cover.

I'd hidden the journal under my mattress in New York, hoping to leave it behind, along with Dr. Deerchuck's other useless suggestions. But it looked like someone had gone mattress diving earlier that day.

"Oh, good," I said, unenthused. "You found it."

"You should find a better hiding spot next time," Dr. Deerchuck said, and winked at me conspiratorially.

"I'll definitely be doing that," I responded, shoving the journal into my backpack and going back to staring out the window.

Thankfully, Dr. Deerchuck got a phone call from some other hysterical patient just then and spent the rest of the ride trying to calm them down. Which meant that for the first time in over a week, I had some time to just think.

Think about how messed up my life had become.

How bizarre it was going to be to live with Uncle Scotty.

How much I missed my dad and our old life.

"Next stop, Greenwich, Connecticut," a man's voice called out dully over the loudspeaker.

"That's us!" Dr. Deerchuck said, clapping her hands down onto her lap enthusiastically.

I stood up on shaky legs, slinging my backpack over my shoulder. As I followed Dr. Deerchuck to the exit, I reached up and played with my bangs nervously.

In preparation for trying to fit in to my new hometown, I'd dyed my previously platinum-blond hair a flat brown and had it cut it into a bob with short bangs.

I've never had bangs before. At least on my *real* hair. I've had wigs with bangs, but I've only ever worn them until the end of a con. I haven't had to *live* with the actual unpredictability of shorn locks. And I pretty much regretted the decision immediately following that first snip. The hairdresser had cut them so short, I now had nothing to hide behind, which made me feel even more noticeable than before.

The whole decision had been pretty much one big, epic fail.

At least it seemed to match my life at the moment.

"Do you think you'll recognize your uncle?" Dr. Deerchuck asked as we stepped off the train and into the midafternoon sun.

The station looked like one of those old-school train stops. Sort of like the one at Disneyland. All bright and shiny and happy. Like you were stepping off into a completely different world.

Which, well, we sort of were.

"Well, hello, ma'am." A middle-aged man with light blue eyes stopped us as the train pulled away behind us. "May I help you and your . . . daughter get a ride into town?"

I frowned. People don't do something for nothing. This guy wanted something, and I wasn't going to fall for it just because he was flashing a perfect set of teeth and kind eyes.

I started to tell him to shove off, but Dr. Deerchuck cut in.

"Well, that's very kind of you, but we're meeting someone," she responded politely.

"Of course," the man replied. "Well, let me know if you need any help with anything."

As the man walked away, Dr. Deerchuck looked sideways at me. "I know it's hard given your past, but not everyone is out to con you," she said to me, gently. "This is a nice town. Full of nice people. My hope is that you'll be able to let your guard down eventually, Frankie."

When I didn't respond, Dr. Deerchuck adjusted her purse back onto her shoulder and started to look around.

"So do you recognize anyone?" she asked, sounding hopeful.

I scanned the platform and then looked beyond it to the parking lot. There were around thirty people bustling around, which seemed busy for a small town in the middle of the day, but what did I know about this place?

Still, I picked Uncle Scotty out almost immediately.

I couldn't see his features from so far away, but my instincts told me it was him. He was the only person standing still, and he was leaning back against an enormous red Ford truck. And his slouch was exactly like Dad's.

And mine.

So I guess we had *something* in common.

He was wearing fitted jeans and what appeared to be a suit jacket, even though it was in the mid-seventies in September. His sunglasses reflected the sun and nearly blinded me as he turned to look in our direction.

As soon as he saw me, he lifted his hand in hello, and I did the same.

"Ah, is that your uncle then?" Dr. Deerchuck asked, squinting as she tried to get a better look at the guy who would be taking care of me for the foreseeable future. "He's not quite what I expected, I must admit."

I nodded.

"Funny, none of this is what I expected, either," I said, and started off toward Uncle Scotty.

Entry Four

Standing there in front of Uncle Scotty was surreal.

It was like looking at a younger, fitter, darker-haired version of my dad. Like what I imagined Dad looked like when he first met my mom. Before he realized that in his line of work, it was better to go unnoticed than to stand out. People remember good-looking.

They do *not* remember unremarkable.

At least, that's what Dad told me whenever I'd make fun of the fact that his gut was starting to hang out over his pants and his disheveled blond hair made him look like Justin Bieber during his breakdown.

"It doesn't pay to be handsome, Frankie," he said once. Then he patted his slightly doughy stomach and ran his hands through his hair. "Don't underestimate the power of plain."

"So *this* . . . ," I said, gesturing grandly to him, "is a *conscious* choice you're making?"

"Hey, I've worked really hard to cultivate a disguise that allows me to remain unnoticed wherever I go," he said, giving me an impish smile. "You, on the other hand . . . you got your mother's devastating looks. That means you're going to have to work extra hard to hide the fact that you're absolutely extraordinary."

"I don't look *that* much like her," I said, waving off the compliment, though I wished it were true.

Because the truth is, my mom was stunning. Like, movie star beautiful. With her long blond hair that swished around the middle of her back and a figure that would make a supermodel jealous, her beauty was only surpassed by her cool-chick attitude. Of course, I don't know this from experience. I was really young when she went away. But everyone who knew her said the same thing: Laney Lorde was a force to be reckoned with.

Over the years, I've often wondered how my mom managed to be as good at the con as she was. If what Dad said is true, people stopped whatever they were doing to stare at her whenever she entered a room. And after years on the job with Dad, I know it's nearly impossible to get away with anything when all eyes are on you.

Then again, I guess that's why Dad insists that Mom was the best in the biz. Her looks had forced her to work even harder at her craft, which made her better than the average thief.

Whenever Dad said I reminded him of her, we both knew he was exaggerating or saying it to make me feel better about myself. Because, while I inherited Mom's blond hair and cheeky attitude, my body still looks like a boy's. I'm all angles and bones. Let's just say I've been wearing a training bra for years now, but the *training* has *not* helped.

Still, the features my mom *did* pass on to me are unusual enough to get me noticed. Thus, the reason I'd opted for a mousy-brown dye job and an Anna Wintour–like haircut for my move to Connecticut. At least it dulled me down enough to ensure that I'd fit in.

Because I had no interest in standing out here. In fact, I planned on doing my time quietly until Dad either got out on parole or broke out—whichever came first—and we could resume our perfect lifestyle of traveling and conning.

Uncle Scotty suddenly cleared his throat, and I startled, the reaction snapping me back to reality. I hadn't realized how long I'd been standing there just staring at him until it was glaringly obvious that I'd been doing so.

"You okay?" he asked me, since I still hadn't said anything.

I shook my head to make the memory fade and cleared the expression from my face.

"Sure, yeah," I said, and then added quickly, "You look the same."

I knew it was a silly statement. Of course he'd changed over the past five years. Everyone changes. But it was also sort of true. Uncle Scotty looked exactly how I remembered him.

"I had a beard for a while," he offered, reaching up to touch his currently smooth face absently. "But I shaved it when it started to get warm out. It was . . . itchy."

16

"Oh," I said, nodding as if I could picture it. But the truth was, I couldn't. I just kept picturing a deranged mountain man with a grizzly beard. Which was so not the clean-cut young cop in front of me.

"Well, *you've* certainly changed," Uncle Scotty said, reaching out and tousling my short bangs awkwardly.

I instantly began to brush them back into place self-consciously, then realized I was fidgeting again and stopped abruptly. It was a new tell for me, and one I wanted to nip in the bud as soon as possible. Tells—things that people unconsciously do that clue others in to what they're thinking and feeling—can give you away. And if Dad taught me one thing, it was to hold all my cards close to the vest.

"Yeah," I said, standing up straighter. "New look for my new life, I guess."

I said this last part mostly for Dr. Deerchuck's benefit, since she was standing right there and probably analyzing our every move. A quick peek out of the corner of my eye proved me right.

Dr. Deerchuck's tell is that she can't hide her emotions. She was currently beaming at me, like I'd just been awarded the Nobel Peace Prize or something. And I knew she was silently congratulating herself on another job well done. I would've rolled my eyes at how easy she was to read, but then I'd be giving myself away too.

And I just wanted to get out of there.

"Well, it looks like everything's going to work out

just fine here," Dr. Deerchuck said, clapping her hands together. "Frankie, what do you think? I can stick around for a while—"

"No!" I said, a little too quickly, before relaxing into a shy smile. This family reunion was going to be awkward enough without having my therapist chiming in on everything we said. "I mean, I think we'll be okay. After we catch up and stuff."

"Okay," she conceded happily. "Well, I'll be talking to you on Tuesdays for our mandatory sessions, but if you need anything before then, you have my number."

I pulled her business card out of my back pocket and held it up for her to see.

"Very well," she said, and turned to Uncle Scotty. "Nice meeting you. Please feel free to reach out with . . . anything that might come up."

"Will do," Uncle Scotty said, shaking her hand in a businesslike way.

I beelined for Uncle Scotty's truck and tossed my bag up onto the seat before Deerchuck could change her mind.

"Is that all you've got?" he asked me as the engine roared to life.

"It's all I need," I said instinctively.

"Right," Uncle Scotty said with a wry smile. "I forgot how much like your dad you are."

I raised my eyebrow at him curiously.

"Is that a good thing or a bad thing?" I asked, figuring his answer would give me some insight into what he was thinking.

Uncle Scotty remained silent for a moment as he put the truck into gear and pulled away from the train station. Just when I thought he wasn't going to answer me at all, he glanced over and gave me a smile.

"I guess it depends on who you ask," he said finally, and pulled out into traffic.

Entry Five

"You hungry?" Uncle Scotty asked me as we drove.

"I could eat," I said, thinking maybe we wouldn't have to talk all that much if we were busy stuffing our faces. "I could use a coffee, too."

Now it was Uncle Scotty's turn to raise his eyebrow.

"You drink coffee?" he asked.

"Dad says—" I started, but stopped when Uncle Scotty began to chuckle.

"Of *course* your dad would let you drink coffee," he said.

I couldn't tell if the comment was meant as a judgment or just a matter-of-fact. The truth is, I've always kind of wondered what Uncle Scotty really thinks of my dad and our lifestyle, considering we're probably the epitome of everything he despises. Well, maybe not *despises*. But let's be honest, our values sort of fly in the face of everything he believes in.

Case in point: Uncle Scotty is a cop, so he must have pretty strong feelings and opinions about staying within the bounds of the law. And while our side of the family is a little more . . . relaxed on the boundaries of right and wrong, it would make sense that Uncle Scotty would be more black-and-white about things.

At least, that's what I've assumed.

Since he's a cop and all.

"It's a myth that coffee stunts your growth, you know," I said. "It's true that it contains caffeine, which stimulates the central nervous system and in high doses can cause anxiety and dizziness and interfere with normal sleep patterns, which can lead to other health issues. But soda and tea have caffeine in them too. So does chocolate. Dad believes in making informed decisions and always thought it was important to let me ultimately choose what went into my own body."

Uncle Scotty looked over at me as I finished my mini-lecture, his mouth hanging open slightly.

I smiled proudly. I love dropping knowledge bombs on people. Especially when they don't see them coming.

"But don't worry, Uncle Scotty," I added before looking out the window again. "I only drink decaf. A girl needs her beauty sleep, you know."

I stared at the scenery as we drove by, taking in every building and house and store I saw along the way. We'd left the train station in one direction, but after a few minutes, I noticed that Uncle Scotty had made a turn and was heading back the way we'd just come.

I notice things like this. Directions we take in cars, paths we go down, addresses and streets we're near at any given moment. It's a tactic that comes in handy, in case you need a quick getaway or have to retrace your steps.

I did it now without even thinking about it. And I

have to admit, the habit serves me well more often than you'd think.

As soon as I realized we were backtracking, there was a small part of me—a part I'd never admit to anyone else—that wondered if Uncle Scotty was taking me back to the train station. Like, he'd already decided I was going to be too much trouble for him and he was cutting his losses early.

Nope, sorry, kid. You're too messed up to fit in with my law-abiding lifestyle. Good luck and see you in another five years, I imagined him saying to me before peeling out and disappearing forever.

But, of course, this wasn't what happened.

Instead, we pulled onto Greenwich.

And it was like arriving in Narnia.

Okay, that's a total exaggeration. It was more like finding myself on the set of *Pleasantville* or *The Stepford Wives,* or in some sort of idyllic buttoned-up town like that. The point was, Greenwich was unlike anywhere I'd ever been before.

And I'd been a lot of places.

Let me set the scene for you: Greenwich Avenue is an interesting mixture of old-school elegance and modern wealth. The one-way street is lined with deep green trees and brightly colored plants hanging from old-school-looking streetlamps. People waved hello to one another as they walked their Labradoodles and Yorkies and Mal-tipoos, or other equally fancy dogs, and browsed the shops along the way. The aforementioned shops ranged from high-end places like Saks Fifth Avenue to Starbucks and stood just a few stories high.

And everything was so . . . *clean.*

Like, I wouldn't have been at all surprised to find men running out of their hiding places to pick up the stray garbage people dropped on their jaunts down the avenue. Then again, I couldn't actually imagine people who lived in this town littering, so perhaps that was the real reason for the strip's pristine appearance.

After a few blocks of this, Uncle Scotty pulled into one of the empty parking spots along the street and turned off the truck.

"You should like this place," he said, pointing to the little café in front of us. "It's worldly, just like you—and it even has coffee!"

I looked over at him to see if he was serious but could tell instantly that he was teasing me.

"Har, har," I responded, rolling my eyes.

"Just want you to feel at home," he said, winking at me.

"Here?" I said before I could help myself. "Not a chance."

The look was only there on his face for a split second, but I caught it anyway: mild disappointment. Or maybe it was sadness?

I couldn't really tell with him yet, and before I could analyze the look any further, he'd replaced it with an easy smile and held the café door open for me.

• • •

As soon as I walked through the doors of Méli-Mélo, the sweet smell of dough and sugar filled my senses and I immediately began to drool. Not noticeably, of course, but enough to make me swallow hard and look around to see what was making me suddenly so hungry.

"Crepes," I breathed as I spied the menu on a nearby chalkboard.

"Did I do good?" Uncle Scotty asked, sounding slightly relieved.

"Very," I answered, nodding as I ventured farther inside the café.

It was obvious that the place was meant to resemble a French bistro, with lots of single tables lining both sides. The walls were painted bright yellow and adorned with colorfully painted canvas. Oversized windows at the front of the store were opened up to let in the fresh air, and a few people sat at the tables and the stools at the counter.

The place wasn't *authentic* French. It couldn't be, since we were in the states, of course. And the real France was somehow both romantically intimate and completely autonomous at the same time. The buildings all held an old-school feel to them, like they hadn't been changed since the day they'd been built, and no detail was left untouched. For instance, every single door was unique and authentic, complete with different designs, shapes, colors, and materials. It sounds like a weird thing to notice—like, who cares about a door, right?—but it really embodied the city itself. No two things were the same in Paris, and nothing was quite what it seemed. I suppose that's the reason I felt so at ease there. Nowhere in the States could compare to that kind of atmosphere—but this café was certainly trying, which made me a bit nostalgic.

And it didn't hurt that it smelled fantastic.

Perusing the menu, I could see that they had a little bit of everything. Soups, salads, sandwiches and crepes—oh, the crepes! Savory, sweet, and everything in between.

I wanted them all.

To be honest, anything would've been preferable to the bland cafeteria-style food we'd been forced to eat at the residential treatment facility I'd been stuck in while my dad was on trial. The sad thing was that the repeat lodgers—i.e. kids who'd been separated from their parents before because of prison stints or trials, and didn't have any other relatives willing to take them in—swore the food where we were staying was better than at child services or most foster homes.

I couldn't see how that was true, but then again, I was a newbie.

Plus, the food was no doubt better than the prison food my dad had been getting. But when you're international foodies like we are, being forced to eat plain chicken, white rice, and a vegetable five nights a week is practically torture.

Uncle Scotty and I sat down at one of the tables near the open windows a few minutes later, our black-and-white number card there to tell our waiter where to bring our food.

"So . . . ," he said once we were settled.

"So . . . ," I answered, because I didn't want to be the one to start this conversation.

"How are you doing?" he asked finally, broaching the subject with what seemed like caution.

"Fine," I answered. "Hungry."

This was what I assumed he wanted to hear. That although all these crazy things had happened to me over the past months and my whole world had pretty much fallen apart, I was holding it together and ready to get on with my life. He didn't *really* want to know about the hard parts. The down-and-dirty details that would make him feel like he had to fix me.

Nobody *really* wanted to know that.

Except for maybe Dr. Deerchuck. But that's her job.

"You know that's not what I meant," Uncle Scotty said softly. "I meant, how are you dealing with all this stuff with your dad?"

Or maybe he *did* want to know all the dirty details?

I hadn't been prepared for that and squirmed in my seat a little.

"I don't know," I said, not really interested in elaborating. "It sucks."

"Yeah," Uncle Scotty said, and ran his hand down his face. "It does."

26

Suddenly he looked tired and stressed. And I started to feel guilty, because I knew at least part of it was my fault.

"Hey, I didn't ask to come here and interrupt your life or anything," I said defensively.

He stared at me, a confused look on his face.

"You're not interrupting my life, Frankie," he explained clearly. "I'm *glad* you're here. I just meant . . . God, this is all so messed up."

I studied him for a few seconds before looking down at the table and laughing out loud.

"You can say that again," I said, nodding in agreement, as our food arrived. I'd ordered both sweet and savory—a crepe with ham and cheese and another with brown sugar, cinnamon, and a whopping dollop of frosting on top. I did a little happy dance in my seat before digging in.

"How's your dad doing?" Uncle Scotty asked, as if the question were a normal one.

I paused, the big bite of ham and cheese filling every inch of my mouth, making it nearly impossible for me to answer. I chewed the best I could and then swallowed, the food burning my throat as it went down.

"He's in prison," I answered bluntly. "How do you think he's doing?"

"Fair enough," Uncle Scotty said evenly. "But are they treating him okay?"

I could hear the concern in his voice, so I held back the response I really wanted to give, which was something to the effect of *He's doing great! They have five-course meals and thousand-thread-count sheets. Prison's like a regular old Club Med!*

"I guess," I said instead, shrugging noncommittally. Then, turning the tables on him, I added, "You haven't talked to him yet?"

"I have," Uncle Scotty admitted. "But he only wanted to talk about you. Wouldn't really give me any details. You know your dad. He's not exactly a talker."

"Mmmm," I answered, and took another bite so I wouldn't have to say more.

"Clearly another trait you got from him," Uncle Scotty answered with a laugh. I knew he meant it as a joke, but it still managed to feel like a dig.

"Maybe he doesn't like to be interrogated," I said.

Another pause.

"Frankie, I'm not trying to interrogate you . . . ," Uncle Scotty began, then trailed off. "I'm just trying to . . . understand what happened."

I'd been waiting for this question from the beginning and still didn't have a good answer for him. But I could tell he wanted one anyway, so I gave him the best explanation I could.

"What happened is, he got caught," I said before getting up and walking away.

Entry Six

I knew he wanted more. But I wasn't ready to give up those details just yet.

First off, I still don't really know Uncle Scotty well enough to divulge all my secrets to him. Second, he's a cop. This alone is enough for me not to fully trust him. Third, I'm not a rat. Loyalty is everything in our line of business, and for all intents and purposes, Dad and I are a team. And you don't give up your partner.

If Dad wanted Uncle Scotty to know about our business, he'd tell him himself.

We spent the ride back to Uncle Scotty's in silence. It wasn't uncomfortable. Well, at least it wasn't for me. My mind was spinning too much for me to worry about what Uncle Scotty was thinking.

How was this living arrangement possibly going to work?

Dad was the one who'd decided I would go and live with Uncle Scotty, so he *had* to have thought it would be a good fit. But we'd only spent a lunch together and I was already questioning whether I could trust Uncle Scotty or not. Dad obviously had. Or he had enough to send me to him, so that meant I should, too, right?

Or was this just another lesson Dad had set up that I

was supposed to learn from the hard way, meant to make me a better thief? Kind of like a final exam? If you can live with a cop and still pull things off, then you're in our special club.

Not that there *is* a special club.

At least I don't *think* there is.

I'd have to ask Dad the next time we talked. And who knew when that would happen, since his phone privileges were constantly changing in his new digs. As it was, I hadn't talked to him in more than a month, since Dr. Deerchuck had thought it would be better to keep our interactions few and far between until after the trial was over. Both for Dad's sake and mine. I think she just didn't want him to interfere with my "progress."

I was hoping that Uncle Scotty would be more open to letting me talk to Dad whenever I wanted. Until then, it seemed like I was stuck here, floundering as I figured out my next steps.

"What the . . . ," Uncle Scotty muttered as we pulled up to his little blue-and-white two-story house.

There on the small porch were boxes. Half a dozen of them, big and small, taking up all the space available on the weathered floorboards. A few packages had been stacked on top of a rickety-looking two-seater swing and looked dangerously close to falling over. A large red trunk blocked the entrance to the house.

Uncle Scotty turned and looked at me dumbfounded.

I shrugged and held back a smirk.

"I thought you said that's all you had," he said, motioning with his head to the single bag next to me on the seat.

"It *was* all I had with me," I said slowly. "At the time."

He cocked his head to the side as if he couldn't believe what I was saying.

"What's a little baggage, right?" I asked sweetly.

Entry Seven

UNCLE SCOTTY'S HOUSE RULES

1. NO LYING.
2. NOTHING ILLEGAL.
3. DINNER IS MANDATORY.
4. THERAPY EVERY TUESDAY.
5. ATTEND SCHOOL.

Kill me now.

Entry Eight

Turns out, Uncle Scotty has his limits, and these are them.

And he laid them out almost immediately after we'd come home to all my stuff piled up on his doorstep. It was the first time since arriving that I'd seen him even remotely frazzled, and to be honest, I found the whole situation very interesting.

"Okay," Uncle Scotty said almost to himself as we sat in his truck. He kept the engine on so the air conditioning could run but put the truck into park and turned to face me. "Okay. *Okay*. Listen, Frankie, I know your dad was probably pretty relaxed on rules over the years . . ."

"He only had one," I said. "Don't get caught."

Uncle Scotty nodded like a bobblehead as he took this in.

". . . Yeah. Well, I want to respect your father's wishes, but the bottom line is that we have rules in this house. Rules that will keep you safe and on the right track," he said, scanning my face for any insight into what I was thinking.

I kept my expression blank.

"Okay," he repeated. "First rule: no lying."

"It wasn't *technically* a lie—" I began to argue.

"It wasn't really the truth, now, was it?" Uncle Scotty clapped back.

I shut my mouth again. I knew I couldn't fully defend my actions, so why try?

"This is really important to me, Frankie. In order for this to work, we need to be able to *trust* each other," he said. "And I can't trust you if you're lying to me. But I *want* to trust you. And I want you to trust me. So from here on out, no lies. No withholding any info, even if you think it's small and doesn't matter. Even if telling the truth is going to get you into trouble. I can't keep you safe if I don't know what's going on. And I know your father. There's no way he let you lie to him."

"I didn't need to," I answered truthfully.

"And you don't need to with me, either," Uncle Scotty said. "But I understand we'll need to work up to that kind of relationship. In the meantime, let's both try our hardest to be honest with each other, okay?"

I sighed. "Okay."

"Good," he said. "Next, I'm not going to ask you to give me the details of what you and your dad did on your travels. Frankly, I think it's better if I don't know. But given the charges against him, I'm going to assume not all of it was legal."

I wasn't about to confirm or deny this, so I chose to look out the window instead.

"But, Frankie, I'm a cop. I can't have my niece—

someone who's living under my roof—running around and breaking the law," he said. "I don't know what circumstances brought your dad to live that kind of life before, but they don't exist now. I can take care of you. My salary is more than enough to pay the bills and give you a good life. There's no reason you have to do any of the stuff you did before."

I refused to look at him as he finished, because the truth was, there was so much I wanted to say to that but couldn't.

"Do you understand what I'm saying, Frankie?" Uncle Scotty asked as I remained silent.

Finally, without turning around, I nodded.

"Great," he said. "The others are all pretty easy. I want us to eat dinner together every night. I know it sounds cheesy, and it's going to take some scheduling on my part to make sure I can get away from work at a reasonable hour, but I want to make sure we're connecting. We have more than five years to catch up on, and I think it'll be nice to eat a meal together."

Dad and I have always eaten meals together, too, so this wasn't too out of left field for me. It *did* make me wonder whether it was something the two of them had done growing up. I vowed to find this out later.

"Fine," I said.

"And you won't even have to worry about my cooking," he answered with a smile. "Because I don't cook. I sort of live on takeout."

"Works for me," I said, liking the sound of family dinners even better now.

"Of course, you have to continue with your therapy with Dr. Deerchuck," he continued. "I won't get involved in this part of your life, but just know that she *will* reach out to me if you shirk on your calls."

I mumbled some not-so-nice stuff under my breath concerning what I thought about therapy, but I knew I wasn't getting out of it and eventually agreed I wouldn't miss the Tuesday phone calls.

"And last, you have to attend school regularly," Uncle Scotty finished. "No skipping, no slacking off."

"School? Uh-uh, no way," I said, waving my arms in a crossing motion in front of me. "I'm not going to school here."

"You *have* to go to school, Frankie," Uncle Scotty said, sounding tired. "It's the law."

"Screw that law," I said, feeling a little crazed. "Dad never made me go to school."

"You weren't getting an education?" Uncle Scotty asked, surprised.

"Oh, I was getting an education," I said. "Just, Dad was my teacher."

"Well, now you have to go to school," he said forcefully. "With *real* teachers and other students your age."

"But, Uncle Scotty—" I started to whine.

"You're not getting out of this one, Frankie," he warned. "Might as well just accept it."

"Arrrgh!" I cried out in frustration as he turned off the truck and stepped out.

He'd only gone a few steps before adding, "And school starts tomorrow."

Entry Nine

I'd like to make something perfectly clear right now: up until this moment, my knowledge of middle school has been limited to what I've seen on TV and in movies. And if that's what it's going to be like, I would sooner pull out all my own eyelashes and walk over hot coals than have to experience it firsthand.

Dramatic, I know. But also true.

I told Uncle Scotty as much as we moved my boxes into the house and up to the bedroom that had been cleared out for me. I explained that I didn't understand why I needed to go, when my system with Dad had been working just fine for the past few years. Uncle Scotty's response was that he wasn't equipped to teach me math and science and creative writing, blah, blah, blah.

"That's funny because Dad was great at it, and *he* didn't even go to a fancy school like Purdue," I baited him, hoping his ego would change his mind.

It didn't.

And that's why I was up all night stressing about having to experience my first-ever day of public school as a freaking *middle* schooler.

And I didn't even *want* to care about any of it. If I was going to be forced to go to school, I wanted to just show up and be me. Not care. Because, who cares about making friends and following the sociopathic hierarchy that makes up middle school? I don't. Who cares about sports and getting good grades and having your intelligence measured by arbitrary things like tests and homework? Not me. So then why had I lain awake all night, staring up at the ceiling of my new room, instead of sleeping soundly?

The answer was: because the flip side of not caring about any of it was that it could make my life *that* much harder.

If I was a hundred percent me at this new school, people would know I was different. And being different meant I'd stand out. And standing out was the opposite of everything I'd ever been taught.

Thieves blend into their environments. It's how they get away with things. It's how they survive.

In a way, it's even a sign of just how good you are at what you do. And I've been trained to be the best.

So while I wanted to *not* care about this whole going to school thing, I also *couldn't* not care.

See the problem?

That was when I realized I had to start looking at this whole thing as a *job* and nothing more.

So at five in the morning, I turned on my laptop and Googled "clothing trends for NYC teens." I might not have known a lot about my new place of residence yet, but I was well aware that since it catered to the mon-eyed elite, there had to be a certain sophistication and elegance to people's personal style. And who's better at creating personal style than a New Yorker?

Now, I'll admit, this was a low point for me, and I just want to say that never in my life have I ever Googled such embarrassing words. I spent a few minutes berating myself for not having spent more time investigating what kids were wearing when Uncle Scotty and I were in town. Was I already going soft? I erased my search history as soon as I'd finished my research just to ensure that the proof of its existence never got out.

But I have an excuse for the madness. I swear. And here it is.

I'm going to let you in on some top secret information here. You should know that this kind of intel is usually completely classified. Only known to people in my line of work. It's sort of the blueprint for how *we* do what we do.

The handbook for thieves, if you will.

And like a good magician, thieves never reveal their tricks.

Except I'm going to here. Because nobody's ever going to read this, except for maybe Dad. And he already knows all my secrets.

The first step to pulling off a job is looking the part. Most of the time, this means fitting in with your mark—whoever they are. If they're into sports, you wear a baseball cap and workout clothes. If your target is the son of a diplomat, you stock up on cardigans and pearls.

Of course, there *are* the occasional exceptions to this rule. For instance, sometimes your way in with your mark could mean being the *opposite* of who they are. This works well on the sheltered goody-goodies. Case in point: a good girl always loves a bad boy.

The idea is to get an in—however you can—with whoever you're conning.

And in my case that meant every student at my new school.

Thus the early-morning Googling session.

Ordinarily, I would've gone straight to my red trunk for my disguise. In fact, it was the first place I went that morning out of habit. But when I opened it up, I was reminded that this was no ordinary job. Which meant it would call for a completely different set of tools. Tools I didn't have. Tools I'd never used before.

Closing the trunk and locking it up tight again, I turned to the boxes that held my regular clothes and sighed.

Usually I had days if not weeks to prepare for a new case. I would even build in time to go shopping for what I needed. But considering my limited time frame, I was going to have to make do with what I already had.

Which for the purposes of this job meant borrowing a pair of Uncle Scotty's too-big-for-me pants out of the dryer— luckily he wore them fitted—and cinching them with a belt at the waist. Then I dug around in my boxes until I found a multicolored tank, which I went at with a pair of scissors, cutting away about six inches of material to reveal just the tiniest sliver of skin between my pants and top.

It was *so* not my style, but that didn't matter. Because it was apparently what was "in" with my new crowd at school, and that meant it was what I'd be wearing for the foreseeable future.

Ugh.

But what can you do? There are times when being a thief isn't easy. This was one of those times, I suppose.

"Hey," I said when I finally slinked down the stairs and fell into a chair at the kitchen table in the morning. Uncle Scotty was standing at the counter, looking at his phone while drinking something from a mug.

A half dozen boxes of cereal sat on the table and an empty bowl and a spoon had been set out for me. I grabbed the unopened carton of milk and filled my bowl before I'd even picked out what I was going to add to it.

"You must *really* like cereal," I said, looking at all my choices.

Uncle Scotty barely looked up from what he was reading. "It's the breakfast of champions," he said absently.

I could tell he never actually ate the cereal himself. None of the boxes had been touched, and a glance over at him showed no empty bowls in his vicinity. It didn't take a detective to guess he usually ate something at the station or skipped breakfast altogether.

As I mulled this over, I chose an organic, gluten-free cereal I'd never heard of before and popped a handful of it into my mouth before adding it to my bowl.

42

"And here I've been missing out on being a champion all these years . . . ," I said sarcastically, taking a big bite and crunching on it loudly.

This seemed to catch Uncle Scotty's attention, and he finally looked up at me. "Sorry?" he said. "Do you not like cereal? Would you rather have bagels or waffles or something? If there's something else you want, just write it down on the notepad on the fridge and I'll pick it up at the store on my way home."

"Cereal's fine," I mumbled, and pulled my leg up next to me in my chair.

Uncle Scotty's expression turned puzzled, and he squinted as he took a closer look at me.

"Are those my pants?" he asked.

"Oh, yeah," I said, throwing my leg out to the side to show him my impromptu fashion choice. "I didn't have time to unpack everything last night and all my stuff is still in boxes. I figured you wouldn't mind, since it would make me late to school if I had to look for something else to wear."

Uncle Scotty opened and then closed his mouth like he was going to say something more, but I cut in.

"I mean, I can go and change, but it would definitely make me late to class. And I don't want to start things off on the wrong foot with my teachers, so in that case, it would probably just be better if I skipped today and started fresh tomorrow . . . ," I rambled, figuring that either outcome would be fine with me at this point.

"No," Uncle Scotty said with a sigh. "You can wear them. Today. But after this, why don't you try to stick to your own clothes? We can go shopping this weekend if you need new stuff."

"Roger that," I said, giving him a little salute.

He gave me a weird look again before turning back to his phone.

"How did you sleep?" he continued distractedly.

"Fine," I said, the word tumbling out before I could stop it. Then I remembered rule number one. Well, if Uncle Scotty wanted the truth, then I'd give him the truth. "Actually, I was kind of up all night stressing about today. So much is changing, and adding school to the mix just threw me off."

Uncle Scotty looked at me sympathetically. "Look, I know things are . . . different here, but I'm just trying to do what I think is right for you," he said gently. "Trust me, school is the best place for you right now. You'll see. You're going to love it."

"Now who's lying?" I said as I pushed back from the table and put my empty bowl in the sink.

Entry Ten

Though I had no concrete proof in the matter, I was pretty sure that showing up on your first day of school accompanied by a police officer was not the way to fit in. And although I kind of liked the idea of people thinking I was some sort of deranged delinquent worth staying away from for the rest of the school year, I also knew it wouldn't help me accomplish my goals of flying under the radar.

So I begged Uncle Scotty to drop me off a few blocks away from Western Middle School instead of escorting me inside.

"I don't know if I like the idea of you walking to school alone," he said, putting on his serious cop face.

"It's just a few blocks," I argued. "And besides, this is *Greenwich*. It's not exactly the big city. What are you afraid is going to happen? That I might catch wealth and privilege?"

I snorted at my own joke, but Uncle Scotty didn't join in.

"Greenwich has crime too," he said. "Otherwise I'd be out of a job."

"Right," I said slowly. I could tell this tactic wasn't working with him, so I changed things up. "Hey, this'll give us a chance to work on that whole trust thing you were talking about. You can *trust* me to get to school okay on my own and I'll trust you that there are bad guys out there I should be looking out for."

I gave him a hopeful smile.

I didn't add that most people would probably consider me and Dad two of those bad guys.

I could tell he was weighing his options as to how to respond, but a quick glance at his watch seemed to make his decision for him.

"Fine," he conceded. "I'm running late today anyway. We'll give this a try, but I reserve the right to change my mind later."

"Deal," I said, not caring about later, as long as he wasn't walking me into school today. Then I added, "Thanks, Uncle Scotty."

He couldn't help but smile at that, and it reminded me that for the most part, Uncle Scotty was a good guy who was just trying to do his best with the cards he was dealt.

Just like I was.

Maybe we were more alike than I realized.

"O-okay," I stammered, not wanting this to grow into a mushy family moment. "Um, wish me luck?"

"Good luck," he said. "But if I know you, you won't need it."

I started to say something sarcastic back but then just waved instead and headed off in the direction all the other students seemed to be going.

As I walked toward the school entrance, I tried my best to sneak peeks at the other kids without them noticing that I was scoping them out. I wouldn't ordinarily have taken the risk of looking like the new girl, but I needed to get a better idea of what I was getting myself into.

In the end, it appeared that Google hadn't completely let me down. The girls were all wearing variations of my outfit. High-waisted pants with cropped tops. Shorts that stopped just below their butts paired with baggy, over-sized shirts. Sundresses with jean jackets and Vans. It was the I'm-trying-but-not-that-hard vibe that I'd seen made popular on every Nickelodeon and Disney show ever.

The guys were less predictable.

Any trend seemed to go with them. From the baggy pants and skater shirts to the fitted jeans and button-downs. Even the skinny jeans and distressed tops had a place in the fashion lineup.

There was literally no imagination anywhere that I could see, and I found myself longing for the boho, dressy-chic style I'd seen in Paris.

I focused my gaze back down at the ground in front of me and followed the horde up the front steps of my new school, noting the lush green grass on either side of the concrete walkway. Kids were gathered under trees to keep from melting in the already-hot sun, while others were practically running for the shelter of the air-conditioned hallways inside.

I was headed straight up the steps like I knew where I was going and did my best to avoid anyone's gaze as I went. If I could just get to the front office before anyone noticed I was there, maybe the whole transition into public school wouldn't be so bad. I could just fly under the radar from day one and coast through all my classes until I could convince Uncle Scotty that school was a terrible idea—

"Let me get that," a voice said, breaking through my thoughts and causing me to nearly stumble into the door that was now swinging open in front of me.

"Oh," I said, surprised. "You don't have to . . ."

"It's my pleasure, milady," the kid said as he flung the door wide open and bowed dramatically to me.

"Um," I said, completely confused by what was happening. I looked around helplessly, but there didn't seem to be any explanation for the boy in front of me. "Okay. Uh, thanks?"

"*No problemo, mamacita,*" he answered, gesturing for me to enter.

I prayed that the embarrassing moment was now over, but as soon as I stepped inside, I could feel the kid slip in after me and match my pace.

"You're looking for the office, right?" he asked. I tried not to make direct eye contact with him, for fear it would encourage him to keep talking.

"It's okay," I said quickly. "I know where I'm going."

It was only partly a lie, but this kid didn't need to

know that. And the truth was, I *did* know where I was going: as far away from him as I could get.

"Really?" he said, cocking his head to the side and looking confused. "But you're *new*."

I'm sure he didn't actually yell this out to everyone within a twenty-foot span, like it felt. But I still cringed at the label and glanced around to see if the other kids were staring at us.

Surprise, surprise, they were.

"I'm fine, really," I insisted, quickening my pace.

But this only made him speed up too.

"You *have* to let me help you," he insisted. "I'm the welcoming committee."

"Seriously?" I asked, surprised. What kind of school had its own welcoming committee? It sort of made me hate the place even more.

The kid had begun to lose his breath trying to keep up with me, but to his credit, he forced his words to come out anyway.

"Okay, so I'm not *officially* the welcoming committee," he admitted. "But I know where everything is around here, and you don't, so I think that qualifies me for the position."

I stopped in the middle of the hallway then, preparing to tell him to back off. But then I looked at him a little more closely—and completely forgot what I was going to say.

Because my tormentor turned out to be a slightly pudgy

kid who appeared to be of Mexican descent, about a foot taller than me with longish dark brown hair pulled to one side and secured behind one of his ears. Not that any of that was enough to make him stand out. It was actually his outfit that made me do a double take. He was wearing bright red skinny jeans and a black V-neck shirt covered by a gray vest. To top it all off, he'd slung a slouchy scarf around his neck and shoulders, despite it not being a bit cold inside or out.

And then as if on cue, my one-man welcoming committee procured a fedora out of thin air, twirled it in his hand, and placed it on top of his head.

My mouth fell open. The move felt completely rehearsed. Like I was possibly on some sort of hidden-camera show. And I had to blink to make sure it had actually happened.

It had.

"I'm Oliver," the kid said finally, holding out his hand to me formally. "But everyone just calls me Ollie. You can call me whatever you want."

It sounded like a lame pickup line, but I wasn't getting that kind of vibe from him.

It was more like . . . he was excited for me to be there?

But that didn't make sense, either, considering that for all he knew I was just some boring loser kid transferring from another school. I'd made sure that nothing about me screamed interesting of any kind, and my humdrum haircut and underwhelming outfit weren't going to alert others to my potential coolness.

So why did he care at all that I was there?

I decided *I* didn't care and had to get out of there.

"I really appreciate the welcome. Really, all of that was . . . *great*," I said, gesturing in his direction. "But I really think I can handle it. Just point me in the direction of the office—"

"Right there," Ollie said pointing directly behind me.

"—and feel free to go back to whatever you were doing before I showed up," I finished.

"Are you sure—" Ollie began.

I held up my hand. "Bye, Ollie."

"Oh," he said, his face falling slightly. "Okay. See you later, uh . . ."

I knew he was fishing for my name, but the less anyone knew about me, the better.

"Later," I said, and turned on my heel to march into the office behind me.

Entry Eleven

There wasn't much paperwork for me to fill out when I finally got into the office. Uncle Scotty had dealt with the majority of it before I showed up, and what was left was me just filling in the blanks on where I was academically. What level math had I been studying before? What books was I reading? How many years of Spanish had I taken so far? Some of the questions were actually fun to answer, all things considered.

I sat silently in a chair across from the main front office worker as she read over the pages I'd filled out. The woman looked like she was about a hundred years old and told me to call her Miss Elloise. She stared at my papers for over five minutes, commenting on things here and there, moving at a pace that matched her age.

"It says you speak four different languages, Miss . . . ," Miss Elloise said, searching for my name on the paper in front of her.

Hint: it was the first thing I'd filled out.

"Frankie Lorde," I offered. "And yes. I can speak French, Spanish, Italian, and English."

"Fluently?" she asked skeptically.

"*Si, Señorita Elloise. Aprendí español primero,*" I said. "*Poi siamo passati all'italiano. Et le dernier endroit ou nous avons vécu était Paris, donc c'était assez facile à trouver."*

I switched from each language without any difficulty as I answered her question. Translated, it meant: Yes, Miss Elloise. We learned Spanish first. Then we moved on to Italian. The last place we lived was Paris, so that was pretty easy to pick up.

Yes, I was showing off a bit, but she was the one who'd asked.

Miss Elloise just nodded and didn't question any of the rest of my answers.

"You have first period with Mr. Misaki," she said finally, handing over a piece of paper she'd retrieved from her printer. The printer, I noticed, moved faster than she did. "Mr. Misaki's class is over in B wing, classroom twenty-eight. Would you like me to escort you there?"

"Uh, no thanks," I said, trying not to make it sound like I thought this was a terrible idea. "I think I can find it."

"Okay," she said. I could sense her appreciation for the fact that she wasn't going to have to move from her chair again anytime soon. "Well then, good luck, Miss Lorde."

After a few wrong turns and one trip to a different wing entirely, I finally found the right building and classroom.

According to the printout of my class schedule, my first-period teacher, Mr. Misaki, teaches literature. At least I won't be starting off each day with a subject I hate. Lit is easy, because I love to read. Doesn't matter what genre, I like them all.

In fact, I've secretly always imagined I'll grow up to write stories. Ones with some sort of mystery in them, like Sherlock Holmes. Or possibly adventure books, where the stakes are high and the payoffs even higher.

Maybe that's why writing in this stupid journal comes so naturally to me. I'm not exactly thrilled to *be* the subject matter, but telling an exciting story? Yes, please.

Taking a deep breath, I walked into class.

The bell hadn't rung yet and only about half the seats were taken, so I spotted an empty chair in the middle and headed for it.

"Miss Lorde?" a deep voice called out from the front of the room, stopping me in my tracks.

"Yes?" I said, turning around slowly to find a thirtyish man standing behind an oak desk looking straight at me.

"Would you mind coming here a moment?" he asked, beckoning for me to join him at the front of the room.

I turned back at the empty chair longingly, then spun and walked the other way.

By the time I'd reached him, the man had taken a seat on the edge of his desk and was leaning back easily. He didn't look like the paunchy old I-hate-my-job-and-my-life teachers I'd seen on TV. Instead, he was bright-eyed and impeccably dressed in a blue and pink plaid suit that appeared to have been tailored to fit him perfectly. An iced green tea sat sweating on his desk, but it had been set down on a coaster so it wouldn't leave a ring.

"The office gave word that we'd be getting a new

student today," he said, breaking the silence. "I'm Mr. Misaki. I'll be *attempting* to teach you literature— depending, of course, on your willingness to learn."

He gave a little chuckle at this and smiled a perfect toothpaste-commercial grin.

"And you're the infamous Frankie Lorde," he said, gesturing to me.

"Infamous?" I asked, beginning to panic.

"Well, you're the mysterious new student at Western, so your presence is a treat," Mr. Misaki announced like it was some sort of school record. "I've always thought that a fresh mind births fresh ideas. I have high expectations for you, Frankie Lorde."

"Oh, goody," I said, not exactly thrilled at being on anyone's radar. Even if it was for a teacher who seemed cooler than most.

"Out of curiosity, what was the last book you read?" he asked, crossing his arms over his chest.

I looked around as other kids began to enter the room behind me and fill in more and more of the seats.

"Uh, let's see," I said, distracted. I wanted to give him whatever answer was going to allow me to sit down faster. And I wasn't quite sure what would leave him unimpressed enough to become bored with me.

But I was also having trouble thinking of any book titles at the moment. I'm usually so good about being put on the spot, too. This whole school thing was throwing me off my game.

"Uh, *The Giver*?" I supplied finally.

"Ah, one of my personal favorites!" he exclaimed. Then he winked at me conspiratorially. "I do believe your former teacher had great taste."

"It wasn't a school assignment," I said before I could stop myself. "It was just for fun."

"Even better!" he said, looking at me more closely. "Well, it's on our reading list for later this year, so you may get a little break from assigned reading during that time if you can recall all the details."

He pulled a piece of paper out of a file folder on his desk and handed it to me.

"In the meantime, here's a list of the books we'll be focusing on this year, along with the dates we'll be studying them. Feel free to read ahead if you choose to, but make sure to brush up before tests," he advised.

I glanced down at the paper and scanned the list:

Number the Stars by Lois Lowry
Where the Red Fern Grows by Wilson Rawls
Eragon by Christopher Paolini
Wonder by R.J. Palacio
Speak by Laurie Halse Anderson
Bridge to Terabithia by Katherine Paterson
Harry Potter and the Sorcerer's Stone
     by J. K. Rowling

These and about a half dozen others made up the eclectic list of novels our class would be expected to read this year. I'd already plowed through more than half of them.

Looks like I'll have a lot of downtime after all. Not that that's a bad thing.

Maybe school won't be the crap hole I thought it was going to be.

The bell rang loudly in the corner of the room. I winced at the noise and began to turn away from Mr. Misaki to go to my desk, but he put his hand on my arm and pulled me back gently.

"Wait just a second there," he said. "I'm not through with you just yet."

I complied as he guided me from his desk to the front of the classroom and deposited me there, instead of at a desk and chair like I thought he would.

"Class, let's all welcome a new student," he said, gesturing to me as I stood there frozen. "This is Frankie Lorde."

Entry Twelve

Every pair of eyes was staring at me. Some in boredom, others with slight interest. The rest seemed to be blank, thank God.

I started to dart toward the only empty seat I could find, in the second row, but Mr. Misaki called me back.

"Miss Lorde," he said, going back to his perch on the desk. "Would you mind sharing a few things about yourself?"

I looked at the class in front of me and blinked.

"Wait, you guys really do that here?" I asked him, shocked that what I'd seen in movies was actually true.

Mr. Misaki looked at me, confused, and it hit me that he wasn't joking. He really wanted me to introduce myself. He gestured again for me to start, and I swallowed and began to speak.

"Um, I'm Frankie," I offered uncomfortably. Then I shrugged, because I wasn't sure what else to say.

I looked over at Mr. Misaki, but he was no help.

So I scanned the rest of the class miserably, hoping that most of the other kids would at least feel my pain and grant me immunity on what was happening. But either the other kids had never had the pleasure of embarrassing themselves publicly or they were perfectly happy to revel in my horror, because I didn't see any sympathy in their faces. Until my gaze fell on one face that I recognized.

Ollie sat in a seat near the window, and as we made eye contact, he held up his thumbs and mouthed, "You got this!"

"Uh—well—um," I stammered, surprised to see him there and momentarily losing my concentration.

Of *course* he would be in this class.

I'd been staring at Ollie so long now that the kids who were paying attention to me began to turn around and stare at him, too. When he realized people were turning to face him, Ollie leaned back in his chair triumphantly and gave them all a little wave.

Oh, God. He's going to make this even worse, isn't he?

I had a horrible vision of him joining me at the front of the classroom and trying to introduce me himself.

No way, uh-uh, not going to happen, buddy.

I immediately forced myself to look somewhere else. Anywhere else.

"Like I said, I'm Frankie," I choked out, trying my best to sound like I was unaffected by what was happening. "I just moved here from Paris. I live on coffee. And, uh, that's pretty much it."

"Well then," Mr. Misaki said when he realized I wasn't going to say anything else. "Why don't you take a seat right there and we'll go ahead and get started."

I practically sighed with relief as I beelined for the only chair that was left open and fell into it gratefully. It might have been second row center, but at least it was far enough away from Ollie that he wouldn't be able to try to talk to me again.

It's not that he's a bad guy. Heck, I don't even know him. But if I'm not careful, a guy like that could easily sabotage my whole plan.

"I believe we left off on June twentieth's entry," Mr. Misaki said, holding up his copy of *The Diary of a Young Girl* by Anne Frank.

I looked down at my desk, nearly expecting a copy to have materialized out of nowhere, but it was empty.

"Miss Valera," Mr. Misaki said. "Would you mind sharing your book with Frankie for now until she can get her own copy?"

"Sure," a striking brunette said beside me. She had hair that went all the way down to her waist, and she was wearing a little yellow tunic that was perfectly pressed and topped off with a crisp white collar. She glanced sideways at me and gave me a polite smile before scooching her chair over to mine and placing the book partially on my desk.

"Thanks," I said gratefully, even though I knew the girl had no choice in the matter.

"It's no problem," she said to me easily.

From his place at the front of the room, Mr. Misaki began to read from the book.

I'd read Anne Frank's diary a few years back when Dad and I had gone on a short trip to the Netherlands. The author had been several years older than I'd been at the time, and for a hot second, I'd thought it would be trés chic to write in a diary like she had.

But then it was pointed out to me—by my dad—that we were only able to read Anne's book because someone else had gotten ahold of her private thoughts and made them public. Even if her intent had been to have it published eventually, everybody in the world now had the ability to read what she'd written.

And that was too big a risk to take, I'd thought. What if somebody found my diary and read it? What if they gave it to a publisher? Or the police? I might as well have handed the government a confession right then and there.

So that put the kibosh on writing in a diary. At least until my therapist insisted I keep one.

I quickly scanned the entry that Mr. Misaki had referenced.

Ahhh, it was the one where Anne muses that nobody would ever want to be privy to the thoughts and feelings of a thirteen-year-old.

And maybe that would've been true if she'd been a normal, boring, typical kid.

But she hadn't been.

And neither was I.

I thought of my black-and-white notebook back in its new hiding space at the bottom of my red trunk.

At least I was in good company. Because now Anne was a legend.

Not that I want that kind of notoriety. In fact, I really hope nobody ever reads this. Or if they do, I hope it's long after I've died so that I can't get in any trouble for the things I might reveal in this journal.

Because one thing's sure, the stuff I do could get me in a lot of trouble if anyone knew about them.

"It's very interesting that at the time, Anne poses the theory that no one could be interested in hearing about what she has to say about life, just because she's a young person," Mr. Misaki says, closing the book. "Especially when we now know that what she had to say held *extreme* relevance in both that particular time period and that place, as well as now in our modern day. In fact, if she had listened to her original instincts, we might have very little knowledge or proof of what it was like for someone in hiding during the Nazis' occupation of the Netherlands. Regardless of her age, this diary is an unflinching representation of a specific time in the world's history.

"For your assignment today, I'd like to pose a question to you," Mr. Misaki continued. "If you were to keep your own diary, what sorts of subjects would it deal with? What is happening in your world now that reflects our society?"

"You mean, like, what's really in lunch lady Esme's meatloaf surprise?" a freckled boy in the back row said loudly.

"There you go, Dustin! Questioning the contents of our food is a very hot topic right now," Mr. Misaki said, nodding. "With more than thirteen-point-five million children and adolescents battling obesity in our country, it would make sense that young people would want to make a conscious effort to pay attention to what exactly is in the food they consume."

"Is BTS better than 1D?" a girl called out next.

"Duh, seven's better than five," another girl answered, looking disgusted by the question.

"But 1D has Harry Styles," the first girl said.

"Who cares!" a blond boy near the front yelled out, rolling his eyes. "They're all a bunch of freaks."

"Now, Brandon, let's not downplay Stacey's question," Mr. Misaki said. "Music can be very influential, and it's worth considering how K-pop and other international singing groups have shaped the way Americans look at other cultures. For instance, what is it about BTS that resonates with young people in the US, when the majority of their music isn't even translated into English? What is it about the group that transcends this language barrier?"

"They're hot," a girl offered.

"They look like girls," Brandon said, sounding even more annoyed than before. "Does that mean you like girls, too, Natalie? You *do* hang out with Jordana a lot. . . ."

The girl named Natalie instantly turned red but narrowed her eyes at her tormentor.

"I *don't* like girls like that," she answered through clenched teeth. "Do you like guys like that? It seems like you're always slapping butts on the field. Maybe you like it a little too much."

"Okay, okay. I'm afraid we're getting a bit off-topic here," Mr. Misaki said, waving his hands in the air. Then his face went thoughtful. "Though a discussion on gender and sexual identity would certainly be relevant in today's world."

A bunch of kids around the class snickered at this, and I found myself rolling my eyes.

Really, people?

I've been all around the world and met so many different people that it seemed crazy to me that anyone would have hang-ups about a person's sexual orientation in the twenty-first century. Gay, straight, bi, trans, who cares as long as love is the goal, right?

Were these really the things that regular kids worried about? Food, boys, music? What kind of place had Uncle Scotty sent me to? I was beginning to wonder if kids were idiots no matter where you went. Wealth and refinement didn't seem to buy you taste—or class, for that matter.

"Let's use this as a starting off point for your writing assignment." Mr. Misaki forged on. "For the next week, I'd like you all to keep a diary. Write down your thoughts, your fears, the things that take up time in your life at this present moment. It can be about anything. Only rule is that it's true to your life."

Mr. Misaki was sounding a lot like Dr. Deerchuck. At least the assignment wouldn't be a stretch for me.

"Ugh," the girl next to me groaned softly as Mr. Misaki dismissed the class a little while later. "What a pain."

I forced a smile. "I know what you mean," I answered. I was going to add that I didn't see how writing our problems down was possibly going to solve them, but something made me hold back. Instead, I said, "By the way, I'm Frankie."

The girl tossed her copy of *Anne Frank* into her bag and swung the black backpack onto her shoulder. The gold Gucci logo shone under the fluorescent lights.

"So we heard," she said, gesturing to my former spot at the front of the classroom. "I'm Annabelle."

She didn't reach out to shake my hand. In fact, she didn't really look at me at all as she introduced herself.

"Who has time to worry about the world's problems?" she continued. "I mean, what about me?"

I started to chuckle but then realized she was serious.

"Oh," I said, swallowing back the laugh the best I could. "I think maybe that's the point?"

Annabelle just stared at me blankly.

"Whatever," she said. "I think it's a waste of time."

I didn't feel like arguing with her, especially when I was inclined to agree with her on journaling, but for different reasons. So I cleared my throat and changed the subject.

"Uh, I have Mrs. Wallstone next period," I said, showing her my printout. "Is her class far from here?"

Annabelle took my schedule and scanned it critically.

"Old Lady Crankypants?" she said, almost to herself. "She's the worst."

"Annie, you coming?" someone called out from the direction of the classroom door. I turned to see a huddle of girls, all equally pretty and properly dressed, studying us intently.

Annabelle held up a single finger, displaying a perfectly rounded baby-pink nail. Then she turned back to me and handed over the paper.

"Just take a right out of here and keep going that way. You'll run into it eventually," she said with a shrug. She took one last look at me, seeming to analyze me closely for the first time. After a moment that lasted a little too long for my comfort, she waved her pink nails at me. "Toodles, Frenchie. Welcome to Western Middle."

She turned on her heel and sauntered over to her group of friends, who all gave me a quick once-over before hustling out the door.

"It's Frankie," I said, even though she was already gone.

"So it is!" a voice said from behind me.

Ollie.

"Cool name, by the way," he said as he appeared by my side like I'd invited him to join me. "Need some help getting to your next class, *Frankie*?"

I cringed as he said my name. He rolled the *r* like there was something fancy about it.

Again, everything he did seemed to have a special flourish. And I wanted my life to be flourish-free.

"Nope," I said quickly. "I mean, thanks, but that girl, Annabelle, just gave me directions."

"Really?" he said, sounding skeptical. "What's your next class?"

"Mrs. Wallstone," I supplied.

"And where did Annabelle say to go?" Ollie asked.

"She said to take a right out of here and keep going until I hit the class," I answered.

"Yep," Ollie said, nodding. "Annabelle was sending you out to the Dumpsters in the back of the school."

I stopped and looked at him dumbfounded.

"What?" I asked, not sure I'd heard him right.

"She sent you to the Dumpsters," he repeated.

"Maybe I just got her instructions wrong," I muttered, following him out the door and looking down the hallway to the right.

Ollie shook his head. "You didn't," he said. "She's messing with you."

"Why?" I asked, thoroughly confused. I hadn't done anything to her.

"That's Annabelle," Ollie said. "She's sort of . . . well, evil."

I let this sink in. Who *did* something like that to a new girl? Were other kids my age really that childish?

"Okay, so how *do* I get to Mrs. Wallstone's?" I asked with a sigh.

"I thought you'd never ask," Ollie said, smiling brightly. Then, with a little hop in his step—I'm not joking, he literally hopped—he turned left and started off down the hallway. "Allow me to show you the way, Frankie Lorde."

"Oh, brother," I said to myself as I reluctantly followed.

Entry Thirteen

When I was finally able to turn on my phone at the end of the day, there was a message waiting from Uncle Scotty.

Uncle Scotty: *Can't pick you up today. Got stuck in court.*

Hey, not being picked up in front of my new school by a member of the police force? Fine by me.

Me: *That's cool. I can find my own way home.*

I didn't really know my way around yet, but the town couldn't be impossible to navigate. Plus, wandering a bit would allow me to do recon on my new home base.

Before I could move forward with my plan, though, another text pinged through.

Uncle Scotty: *Just meet me at the courthouse.*

101 Field Point Road. If you Uber, I'll pay you back.

If you walk, be careful.

I wanted to respond with an eye-roll emoji but held back. At least he was giving me the freedom to walk there by myself. That already was a big step up from when I'd first arrived.

Must be an important case if he was willing to miss out on the opportunity to come and get me himself.

I plugged the courthouse's address into my phone, then placed my earbuds in my ears and waited for the music to take over my mind.

I definitely needed the distraction after the day I'd had.

Let's just say things had not gotten any better after Annabelle's little "misdirection" that morning. Besides Ollie, barely anyone spoke to me. Which was honestly fine. Preferable, even. But it meant that I spent most of my free time searching for my next class alone and resembling a chicken with her head cut off as I did so. And because of this, I was late to most of my classes. Which seemed to annoy my teachers a bit.

For instance, when I was three minutes late to math class on account of getting turned around in the school's labyrinth of hallways, the math teacher, Mr. Piedmont, made me answer a riddle he'd learned on some math nerd fansite before I could sit down.

"If you buy a rooster for the purpose of laying eggs, and you expect to get three eggs each day for breakfast, how many eggs will you have after three weeks?" Mr. Piedmont wrote the riddle in big script letters on the dry-erase board behind his desk. Then he leaned back in his chair and placed his feet up on his desk triumphantly to await my answer.

The answer was zero, of course. Roosters don't lay eggs.

But I wasn't about to let him or the other kids in the class know I had the answer. Instead, I played dumb as the teacher confirmed what I already knew, and quickly took my seat.

Better everyone underestimate me than know the truth: They have no idea what I'm capable of.

Uncle Scotty, however, does—well, for the most part. That's probably why he'd rather I met him at the courthouse after school than be left to my own devices at home. Alone.

I took my time walking there. For as much as I hated being stuck in this town, I couldn't deny its beauty. Flowers were blooming. Lawns were perfectly manicured. The air smelled awesome. And the weather this time of year was near perfect. Not unbearably hot like the summer, but a delicious shade of warm.

Even at my leisurely pace, it only took me twenty minutes to get to the courthouse. And when I arrived, I was sort of taken aback by the sheer size of the building. I'd expected something smaller. Something that would reflect the small-town feel that Greenwich had. But I was beginning to realize that there might be more to the place than what I'd experienced so far.

The outside walls were gray and white, with a few strips of red brick peppered in for a little shot of color. The courthouse stood three stories high, looming over the lush green trees planted directly in front of the entrance.

It certainly wasn't the largest courthouse I'd seen. That would be the one that I'd stepped into every day for two months during my dad's trial. Apparently when you reach the notorious international thief status that my dad had, they set you up at the biggest, baddest courthouse in NYC in order to find you guilty. The place was a behemoth of a structure, more like a monument than a courthouse. I'd been surprised at first, thinking the fanfare didn't befit his crime, but obviously the dozens of people who'd worked on the case for years disagreed. It's no surprise that after that, any other courthouse would pale in comparison. Still, while smaller in size, the building I currently stood in front of managed to pull off its own intimidation factors.

Walking up the steps, I couldn't help but start to sweat. It was kind of a Pavlovian response, really. Force a thief into a law-and-order situation and they tend to get all itchy.

Put simply: if I never have to step inside another courtroom in my life, I'll die happy.

Guess I'll have to work extra hard not to get us caught next time.

I asked the woman at the information desk where courtroom 23c was, then made my way there, refusing to meet anyone's eyes as I went. I still hadn't bothered to take out my earbuds, and I shook my head ironically as "Smooth Criminal" by Michael Jackson began to play.

I swear, it was just too perfect.

When I got to the room that Uncle Scotty had texted to me, I slowly opened the heavy wooden door and slipped inside as soundlessly as I could. But even though I was operating in super-stealth mode, most of the people in the room turned to look at me. Including Uncle Scotty, who was perched on the edge of the second-row bench.

He made an almost imperceptible motion for me to join him before turning back around to pay attention to the person giving her testimony.

I quickly and quietly tiptoed to the second row and slid into the open spot next to Uncle Scotty. Then, turning off my phone, I finally pulled the buds out of my ears and was able to hear what was being said on the stand.

"Mrs. Martinez, please recount the things that needed to be fixed in your apartment to make it habitable," a woman dressed in a smart blue skirt suit said as she stood a few feet away from what I assumed to be her client.

"*Sí*," the woman on the stand began, then continued in English with a Hispanic accent. "There was wires coming out of the walls, and a ceiling that would spark when you turn on lights. Once my husband got a jolt when the light went on. There were also *roedores*—rats—all over the house and in the walls. You could hear them scratch, scratch, scratch all night long. And no heat all winter. We had to put blankets over the *ventanas* to keep from freezing."

"And did you ask the property owner, Mr. Miles, to fix this?" the female lawyer asked.

"*Sí*," Mrs. Martinez said.

"How many times?" the lawyer asked.

"*Quatro* or *cinco*," she answered.

"So you asked Mr. Miles four or five times to make your apartment *livable*," the lawyer continued.

"*Sí*."

"And what happened next?" the lawyer asked.

"Nothing," Mrs. Martinez said, shrugging helplessly.

"Nothing?" the lawyer asked, like this was the shock of the century and they weren't in court for that very reason.

"No," Mrs. Martinez said. "Nobody ever called. Nobody came by."

"So what did you do next?" the lawyer asked, seeming genuinely interested despite the obvious fact that she already knew what her client had done next.

"We did not pay," Mrs. Martinez said.

"You mean you didn't pay your rent," the lawyer corrected.

"*Sí,*" Mrs. Martinez said. "The Internet says they do not fix, we do not pay."

"Well, that sounds fair to me," her lawyer said as she walked back to her table and sat down. "Your witness, counsel."

Mrs. Martinez's eyes darted over to the defense table nervously. You could tell she wasn't one for confrontation, and the fact that there was a whole table of confrontation about to be focused on her had her visibly shaken. One of the men wearing an expensive-looking suit stood up from his table slowly, then placed his hand over his chin and stroked it thoughtfully as he began to creep toward the stand.

"Good afternoon, *Seniora* Martinez," the man said, giving her an exaggerated grin. "*Cómo estás?*"

74

He'd barely even spoken and already I didn't trust the guy. He was a snake. He looked like a snake. He moved like a snake. His tongue was already wagging like a snake's. He might be nice now, but I'd seen enough to know he was going to strike soon. And poor Mrs. Martinez wouldn't even see it coming.

"Fine," Mrs. Martinez responded guardedly.

"Good, good," the lawyer said, as if to himself, before continuing. "It sounds like there were a lot of things wrong in your apartment, and I'm sorry you had to live like that. But isn't it true that in your lease agreement, it states that tenants are required to make their own repairs above the first one hundred dollars for basic maintenance paid by the management company?"

"*Sí*, but the rats were there when we moved in and we didn't know the heater was broken until it was winter—"

"How do you know the rats were there before you moved in?" the lawyer asked.

"Because we saw the *heces*—uh, *poop*," Mrs. Martinez said.

"If you'd seen evidence of rodents from day one, why did you move in?" the lawyer asked as if this were an obvious question.

"We had already signed the papers and if we backed out, we would have lost our deposit," Mrs. Martinez explained, flustered. "And we had nowhere else to go."

"But obviously nothing was so bad that you felt like you couldn't move in, correct?" The lawyer pushed forward.

"I mean, I wouldn't move into a place after seeing obvious problems like this."

"We thought Mr. Miles would fix it," Mrs. Martinez explained, then looked over at the judge pleadingly. "It was not our fault."

"Do you have proof, Mrs. Martinez?" the lawyer asked, ignoring the woman's distress.

After a second's hesitation, she nodded. "*Sí,*" she answered, gesturing to her lawyer. "We have pictures and video of all the problems we had."

"But none of that proves that the so-called problems existed *before* you moved into the apartment, correct?" the lawyer asked.

"There are pictures," Mrs. Martinez said again, as if that were all the proof she needed.

The lawyer nodded. "I've seen them, Mrs. Martinez," he acknowledged. "And that's why I know that they are time-stamped from just a few months ago. Not from the time you first moved into the apartment. Is that correct?"

This time Mrs. Martinez remained silent.

"So you don't actually have any proof that the rodents were in your apartment *before* you moved in. You don't have proof that any of these problems happened prior to your moving in, in fact," he said, waving his arms around grandly.

"I told them about the rats," Mrs. Martinez said, angry now. "I told them about the wires. I told them right after we moved in."

"Again, where's your proof?" the lawyer asked. He made a show of going over to his table and riffling through the stack of papers, and came back empty-handed. "There's no proof of these so-called complaints, is there?"

"We were told to fill out the repair request forms on the website," Mrs. Martinez said, folding her arms over her chest defensively. "We did. Nothing was fixed."

"Maybe you did," the lawyer said, nodding, though his tone conveyed his disbelief. "But then why didn't my client receive your request?"

"He should have," Mrs. Martinez said.

"I agree," the lawyer said quickly. "Because if he *had* received your *alleged* four or five complaints, he might have been able to help you. But he didn't."

Mrs. Martinez narrowed her eyes at the lawyer.

"I don't believe you," she said firmly.

"Well, you don't have to, Mrs. Martinez," the lawyer said finally. "Because the truth is, there is no proof that those messages were ever delivered to Mr. Miles. He certainly has no record of them. Why didn't you try contacting Mr. Miles another way?"

"We were told the management would only fix repairs if we went through their website," Mrs. Martinez said.

"I'm sorry, but I just find that hard to believe," the lawyer said, suddenly laughing. "If I'd sent a bunch of messages to my landlord and wasn't hearing anything back, I would most certainly give them a call. Did you call them, Mrs. Martinez?"

"I tried to, *sí*," she answered.

"You *tried*?" the lawyer asked. "How many times? Once, twice—"

"Twice maybe," Mrs. Martinez said. "Nobody answered and I couldn't leave a message."

"So living conditions in your apartment were so bad that you could barely stand to stay there, yet you only tried calling your landlord twice to have things fixed? It doesn't sound like it was all that urgent, Mrs. Martinez."

"That's not true!" Mrs. Martinez snapped.

"And then you just stopped paying your rent." The lawyer pushed on. "You had a contract to pay Mr. Miles for living in his apartment complex and you went back on your word. Can you blame him for asking you to move out?"

"He didn't ask, he kicked us out of our home!" Mrs. Martinez shouted.

"The home you so badly didn't want to leave? The same home with rats and dangerous electrical wires and no heat? I'm sorry, Mrs. Martinez, that just doesn't make a whole lot of sense to me."

"They forced us out when we asked them to fix what was wrong!" Mrs. Martinez said, standing up and banging her tiny fist on the stand in front of her.

"Please remain calm, Mrs. Martinez," the judge said quietly before relaxing back into his chair. "Or I'll have to find you in contempt."

Mrs. Martinez's cheeks turned red as she realized

she'd let the lawyer get the best of her. She sat down again and folded her hands in her lap.

"It's all right, Your Honor. That's all I have for this witness," the lawyer said finally, sauntering back to his chair and sitting down with a confident look on his face.

"Thank you, Mrs. Martinez, you may sit down now," the judge said.

As the older woman rose slowly to her feet, I felt my anger rise. I've been all around the world and seen different levels of underprivileged people. Kids who didn't have access to an education. People who slept on mats on cold floors and considered having a roof over their heads a luxury. Yet here we were, in one of the richest towns in one of the richest countries in the world, and we weren't just *not* helping those less fortunate, but some people were actively trying to bring them down.

It made me wonder why my dad was sitting in prison and this guy was wandering around free to destroy other people's lives.

"I would now like to call to the stand Detective Scott Lorde," Mrs. Martinez's lawyer said loudly for all to hear.

Then I watched in awed silence as my uncle got up and headed for the stand.

Entry Fourteen

As Uncle Scotty got up and walked to the stand, I studied the judge to see if he'd bought any of the defense's bull. I certainly hadn't. But then again, maybe it takes a swindler to recognize one. It seemed so obvious to me that the landlord had made it impossible for these people to get repairs done. And for what? To save a little money? From the sound of it, Mrs. Martinez was living in nastiness begin with. So would a few repairs really break the bank for Mr. Miles?

"Do you swear to tell the truth, the whole truth, and nothing but the truth?" the court officer asked as he swore Uncle Scotty in.

"I do," Uncle Scotty answered.

Mrs. Martinez's lawyer got up and approached the stand.

"Detective Lorde," she began, her voice friendly and approachable. "You've been investigating Mr. Miles for some time now, haven't you?"

"I have," Uncle Scotty confirmed, nodding.

"Can you tell us why?"

"I began to hear from citizens several years ago that while they were living in a few specific properties in the southwestern corner of town, they were being made to live in horrible conditions," Uncle Scotty said. "These same residents were then either evicted or threatened when they requested repairs be made."

"So you began to investigate?" the lawyer asked.

"Yes," Uncle Scotty said. "It's not right that lower-income housing should come at the cost of a person's safety and well-being. And there were clearly laws being ignored here."

"Objection," the opposing counsel interjected loudly. "Mr. Miles has not been found guilty of any lawbreaking. Move to strike."

"Just because we haven't charged him doesn't mean he isn't breaking the law," Uncle Scotty argued.

"Sustained," the judge said.

"Detective Lorde," Mrs. Martinez's lawyer continued, "what did you find in the course of your investigation?"

"I found that Mr. Miles was forcing these people to live in deplorable states," Uncle Scotty replied. "When I went to see what was going on myself, I was appalled."

"How so?" the lawyer asked.

"As Mrs. Martinez mentioned, most of the apartments in this area were severely run-down. There were cockroaches everywhere. Exposed wiring, holes in the drywall, leaks, mold. Most appliances that the buildings *did* have didn't work. Heaters, air-conditioning units, refrigerators, stoves, plumbing . . . it was all broken-down."

"I'd like to show some photos that Detective Lorde

took on one of his early visits to some of these dwellings," the lawyer said, and began to press buttons on a remote control she had in her hand.

A photo popped up on a screen already set up in the corner of the courtroom. It was of a kitchen. A dirty kitchen. It wasn't dirty because there were dishes piled up or anything. It was just generally gross. The corners of the turned-up linoleum had a brownish-yellowish tint. The oven was so old, I'd guess it hadn't been in use since before I was born. The wallpaper was peeling in places, completely gone in others. There were large chunks taken out of the wall and you could clearly see through to the wiring inside.

She flipped to the next photo, showing several large rats huddling in the corner of what I assumed was the living room. Nearby were droppings that the rodents had left behind, creating a nice little pile of crap in the person's house.

At least the rats were trying to keep it all in one place.

The next photo showed a bunch of dead cockroaches hidden behind a toaster that had been pulled away from the wall. The shot was so vivid, I could almost imagine one of them still kicking its tiny bug legs until it finally died.

All of it was shocking. And disgusting. And I couldn't believe anyone would live in a place like that.

Or more pointedly, that they *had* to live in a place like that.

Even at our most frugal times, Dad and I had never had to take a room in a roach motel. Obviously, we'd had to build our way up to robbing palaces and estates. In our early years of conning, we primarily lived off one job a year, which might just bring us enough to scrape by on what would be considered a modest living to normal people. And even when money began to dwindle down to nothing, I'd never had to share a space with a rodent or bug.

Well, except for when we lived in New York briefly, but that was only when we rode the subway. And in that case, it was part of the city's charm. At least that's what a true New Yorker would tell you.

What I was seeing here was like a horror movie. And totally not right. Especially in a town like this.

I glanced over at the defendant, Mr. Miles, for the first time.

He was sitting between two suited-up men, wearing a dark blue suit himself, with an even darker blue tie wrapped around his neck like a noose. His face was tan, like he had a season pass to a tanning salon, and his skin looked leathery around the edges.

His blond hair was thick and swooped up and back toward the crown of his head, revealing eyes that looked a little too tight for his age. I'd heard of women getting plastic surgery but had never seen it on a man before. The effect bordered on creepy. Like when you see a zombie. At first they look normal, humanlike even. But when you look closer, you can tell something's off.

That was the vibe I was getting from Mr. Miles.

Full-on zombie.

He was leaning as far back in his chair as he could get without fully reclining and had a big fake smile plastered across his face like this was all a joke to him.

But for Mrs. Martinez, it was her life.

And for that alone, I couldn't help but hate the guy.

"And was this what all the apartments were like when you visited?" the lawyer asked Uncle Scotty.

"Yes," he answered, nodding. "Some were worse, but I figured these pictures were proof enough."

"And you're looking into Mr. Miles for other criminal activities, correct, Detective Lorde?" the lawyer asked.

"Right," Uncle Scotty said.

"Objection," Mr. Miles's lawyer said. "Relevance?"

"It goes to show that Mr. Miles has a history of cutting corners and breaking the law. His past misdeeds can be used to establish a pattern of this sort of behavior," Mrs. Martinez's lawyer argued.

"Your Honor, introducing any other ongoing investigations that may or may not be underway would prove unjustly prejudicial to the proceeding at hand," Mr. Miles's lawyer said.

"Sustained," the judge answered without hesitation.

I made eye contact with Uncle Scotty then and saw him purse his lips in frustration.

"In your opinion, Detective Lorde, has Mr. Miles acted negligently and fraudulently when it comes to the tenants living in this part of town?" Mrs. Martinez's lawyer asked.

"Objection," the other lawyer said.

"Yes," Uncle Scotty said loudly, ignoring Mr. Miles's lawyer. "Absolutely."

"Objection! Detective Lorde isn't in the position to give his opinion in this matter, given that his background is not in real estate law," said Mr. Miles's lawyer.

"Sustained," the judge said again. "Stick to the facts, Mrs. Kinnigan."

Looking disappointed, Mrs. Martinez's lawyer closed her mouth tightly and made her way back to her table.

"No more questions then, Your Honor," she said, sitting down in her chair.

"Your witness, counsel," the judge said.

This time, Mr. Miles's lawyer dispensed with the pleasantries he'd afforded Mrs. Martinez. In fact, he didn't even smile as he made his way over to Uncle Scotty, stopping only a few feet from him.

It didn't matter, though, because Uncle Scotty didn't look all that pleased to be talking to him, either.

"Detective Lorde," the lawyer started, barely containing a sneer. "You alleged before that my client threatened those of his tenants who came forward with complaints. How exactly did he do that?"

"Some he threatened to evict," Uncle Scotty said.

"Which is well within his right as a landlord to do if the tenants don't live up to their part of the contract, is that correct?"

"Yes, but—" Uncle Scotty began.

"Thank you," the lawyer said quickly. "And besides eviction, what other so-called threats did he make?"

Uncle Scotty hesitated before answering. He looked conflicted as he struggled to decide what to say next. I leaned forward in my seat, enthralled.

"Detective Lorde, I'll ask you again," the lawyer said forcefully. "In what other ways did Mr. Miles threaten his tenants?"

Uncle Scotty's words came out almost painfully. "He said he would get some of them deported."

"Ahhh," Mr. Miles's lawyer said, holding up his finger like a lightbulb had gone on. "So what you're saying is that when Mr. Miles became aware that certain residents of his buildings were *illegally* living in the United States, he decided to do the *right thing* and turn them in? I'm sorry, but I don't see the problem here. By definition, these people are breaking the law. Maybe instead of putting Mr. Miles on trial, we should be giving him an award."

"Objection," Mrs. Martinez's lawyer said. "Does counsel actually have a question here?"

"Withdrawn," Mr. Miles's lawyer said, satisfied with himself. "I'm finished with this witness, Your Honor."

With a look on his face that could only be described

as thinly veiled murderous rage, Uncle Scotty got up from the bench and stalked back over to me. Sitting down with more force than was needed, he put his hands on either side of the wooden seat and gripped it tightly.

His knuckles turned white. His face, however, was bright red.

Entry Fifteen

"He's gonna get away with it," I said, shaking my head.

Uncle Scotty and I were sitting at a booth in an old-school pizza place not too far from the courthouse, and while I could tell he didn't want to talk about what had just happened, I couldn't help bringing it up.

"I hope you're wrong, kid," he said, taking a bite of his pizza. "But the judge has all the evidence. Now we just have to hope he does the right thing."

I snorted.

"Like *that's* gonna happen," I said sarcastically.

Uncle Scotty looked at me sideways.

"Why do you say that?" he asked.

"Um, because he's clearly in Mr. Miles's pocket," I answered like it was obvious.

"Based on what evidence?" Uncle Scotty asked, narrowing his eyes at me. "And how do you even know about stuff like that?"

I raised an eyebrow at him.

"Oh," he said, reality kicking in. "Right. Well, even so, what makes you think they're working together?"

I set my slice back down on the paper plate and wiped my hands with a napkin.

"First off, every time Mr. Miles's lawyer objected to

something Mrs. Martinez's lawyer said, the judge sided with Miles," I said, holding up one of my fingers.

"Not every—" Uncle Scotty began to argue.

"Every. Single. Time," I said slowly.

Uncle Scotty seemed to think about this a minute before exhaling loudly.

"What else?" he asked.

"Second, the judge is scared of Mr. Miles," I said, holding two fingers up in the air.

"Scared?" Uncle Scotty said. "Why would a judge be scared of a landlord?"

I shrugged. "Don't know," I said. "Maybe because Mr. Miles is more than just a landlord. Didn't they call him a real estate mogul in there at some point? Mogul means money. Money means power. And power corrupts. My guess is Mr. Miles has some dirt on your judge that he's threatening to let out if he doesn't side in his favor. Or maybe he's being paid off for his verdict. I don't know, but the reason doesn't really matter. Point is, the judge is scared and is going to side with them."

"It's a nice theory, Frankie, but there's no way you can prove any of that," Uncle Scotty said.

"Sure I can," I said easily.

Uncle Scotty looked at me skeptically.

"How?" he challenged.

"Come on, Uncle Scotty. It's *so* obvious," I said.

"Not to me," he said, leaning back in his seat. "So enlighten me."

"Okay," I said. "Well, for starters, the muscles right under the judge's eyes were quivering, like, practically the whole time he was up there."

"Quivering?" Uncle Scotty asked doubtfully.

I nodded. "Like a nervous twitching, almost," I said. "That area of the face is highly susceptible to stress, so it's a clear indicator of fear or anxiety. I guess that's why it's called a nervous twitch."

Uncle Scotty nodded as he took in this information. "But that doesn't necessarily mean he was nervous about Mr. Miles. Or even this particular case, for that matter. For all you know, he could've had a fight with his wife before going to court and was stressed about that."

"True," I conceded. "But that's why you have to take all the other stuff into account."

"Like . . . ," Uncle Scotty prompted.

"Like the darting eyes," I answered. "Every time Mr. Miles's lawyer objected to something, the judge's eyes darted over to Mr. Miles. Not to the lawyer who was objecting, but to Mr. Miles himself. And then the last few times, he just kept his eyes trained on the top of his desk while he said 'Sustained.' He was totally avoiding Mr. Miles's gaze. When a person does that, it usually means that the person they're avoiding is unlikable or that they're feeling some sort of shame about them."

I glanced up from my piece of pizza to see Uncle Scotty looking at me in awe.

"There were a half dozen other indicators, but I don't want to bore you," I said, waving them off. "Just trust me, the judge is ruling in Mr. Miles's favor."

"I didn't notice any of that," Uncle Scotty said, almost to himself.

"You sort of have to be looking for it," I said.

"And you were?" he asked. "Looking for that stuff, I mean."

"Always," I said without thinking. "It's sort of habit by now."

"Another trick your dad taught you?" he asked.

I nodded, even though we both already knew the answer.

Uncle Scotty began scratching his cheek absently as he looked off into the distance.

"Like that, for instance," I said, pointing at his hand. "You doing that. I can tell that you're wondering if I'm reading you all the time."

Uncle Scotty froze as I said this, then quickly placed his hand in his lap.

"Are you?" he asked.

"Not *all* the time," I lied.

"Great," Uncle Scotty said with a sigh. "I'm living with a human lie detector."

"But I'm loads of fun at a party," I said.

"Awesome," Uncle Scotty said, chuckling. "I'll keep that in mind."

We fell into a thoughtful silence as we resumed eating

our pizza and let what I'd just revealed sink in. Finally, after a few minutes, I couldn't hold it in any longer.

"So what are we going to do?" I asked him.

"Tonight?" Uncle Scotty said, confused. "I thought we'd just go home. Don't you have homework or something? Or some unpacking to do?"

"I'm not talking about when we leave here," I said, rolling my eyes. "What are we going to do about the *trial*?"

"We're not going to *do* anything about it," Uncle Scotty said, throwing his napkin down onto his empty plate. "Trial's over. Well, until the judge comes back with a verdict."

"I think we've established how *that's* going to turn out," I said. "But that can't be it. If we know Mrs. Martinez isn't getting a fair shake, what are we going to do to fix it?"

"Nothing, Frankie," Uncle Scotty said softly. "This is our justice system. Perfect or not, we have to trust that everything is going to work itself out."

"But doesn't it piss you off that Mr. Miles is going to get away with it?" I asked, getting fired up. "'Cuz it pisses me off."

"Language," Uncle Scotty warned lightly. "And if he *does* get off, then of course I'll be disappointed, but I'll accept it. I have to. That's my job."

"But that's not fair," I said, sounding every bit my age for once.

"No, it's not," Uncle Scotty agreed. "And life isn't always going to seem fair. During those times, you just have to deal with it, move on, and try harder next time. I think justice has a way of balancing itself out over time. Even if it doesn't happen now, I bet Mr. Miles gets what's coming to him eventually."

"And that would be . . . ," I prompted, pushing him a little further than he seemed to be willing to go by himself. "I just mean, besides being a total jerk and all the slumlord stuff, what else do you think he's done?"

Uncle Scotty remained silent for a few moments as he thought about this. I could tell he was weighing how much to reveal to me.

"I mean, they mentioned at the trial that you're investigating Miles for other stuff, too. What could be worse than kicking an old lady out of her home?"

"Trust me, Frankie," Uncle Scotty said, finally looking at me, a distressed expression suddenly on his face. "A person can do a lot worse than that. And Christian Miles? Well, he's done it all."

I got the vibe that Uncle Scotty had said all he was going to say on the subject for now, but even with the limited details, it was enough to convince me something more had to be done.

"Well then, I hope you're right and he *does* get what's coming to him," I agreed. Under my breath I added, "Even if I have to do it myself."

Entry Sixteen

This is where the story starts to get . . . gray. Like, when people say things are black-and-white? This next part is in that shady gray area. So if you're reading this—which you shouldn't be, because this is my personal journal and not meant for public consumption—you need to make a decision right here, right now.

You can keep reading.

But it's at your own risk.

Because I'm pretty sure that knowing what happens next can make you an accessory after the fact.

Or something equally serious.

So close this journal now. Put it back where you found it and you *might* not go to jail.

This is your last chance.

⋮

v

Okay, well, don't say I didn't warn you.

Entry Seventeen

Uncle Scotty was right about one thing. I *did* have homework to do, and if I didn't want to keep wearing my uncle's clothes, I needed to unpack all my stuff.

And that literally took up the rest of my night after Uncle Scotty and I got home from pizza.

Learning was fun with Dad. He was always clear on how I'd be using the information out in the real world, and that made sense to me. It never seemed like a waste of time, because there was a reason for everything he taught me.

I doubt anyone at my new school could tell me when and how I will *ever* need to do long division. Hello? I have a cell phone *and* a calculator. And don't give me the lame excuse of "But what if all the power goes out in the world and you don't have the use of electronics anymore?"

Come on, people, if that happens, we've got more important problems than me not knowing how to do long division. And if that's a serious concern anyway, then why aren't schools teaching us how to create those electronics in the first place, so we can fix them when the whole world blacks out?

Just saying.

Anyway, after doing my stupid long division assignment

and a few others I could've argued the validity of for hours, I dove into unpacking.

And despite the fact that I probably have fewer clothes than your average girl my age on account of Dad and me living a bit of a nomadic life, it still took me hours to get everything out of boxes and hanging or stored in the right place.

When I'd finished, it was nearly midnight and I was finding it hard to keep my eyes open.

Needless to say, I hadn't had any time to start researching my next target:

Mr. Miles.

And yes, Miles *is* going to be my next mark.

I suppose it's probably strange to *normal people* that I'd decide to do another job so soon after what happened with my dad. Especially considering it left my dad in prison. And the whole promising my uncle that I-wouldn't-do-anything-illegal-while-living-with-him stuff. But for someone like me, giving up the life completely is not an option.

Sure, I've learned from the mistakes Dad and I made. And I certainly understand the stakes now, much more than I did before. But take a break?

No way.

The truth is, stealing is in my blood. It's life. Without it, I have no idea who I am.

But I *am* willing to grow as a thief. Maybe change up a few things for the sake of all my new circumstances.

And that's where Miles comes in. Because his case is different.

Or at least it will be once I get started.

• • •

So as soon as I got to school, I raced to the library and commandeered a computer in one of the back corners. Sure, I could've looked everything up on my phone, but that's like Thieving 101.

You never leave electronic evidence of any job if it can be traced back to you.

Because as I learned through Dad's trial, and years of him drilling it into my head, the government *will* get records of every site you've ever visited on your personal devices and every Google search you've ever done.

And once they have that, you might as well just confess to everything.

So using the school's computers to do my research was pretty much a no-brainer. Nobody would ever be able to trace any of it back to me. That's if anyone found out there was something to trace in the first place. But better to be safe than sorry.

With a quick glance around to make sure nobody was within peeking distance, I Googled Mr. Miles.

And got more than 100,000 results.

Here's something you should know about most rich and famous people. They can be incredibly stupid. For instance, a lot of them like to brag about how much money they have or the dumb things they buy with said money. They do this in the media. They open up their doors to magazines, television, newspapers—pretty much anyone who will listen to them talk about themselves.

And the problem with this is that it's basically inviting us thieves to come and rob them blind. Actually, if I'm being honest, it comes across more like they're *challenging* us. And a challenge to a thief is what we live for.

Hey, it's not like I'm complaining. When rich people do these interviews and profiles, it just makes it easier for us to do our jobs. Sort of like they're doing all the prep for us. I just sit back and let them tell me everything I need to know.

And it's for this exact reason that I don't feel bad about stealing from them. After all, they've pretty much handed me the blueprints to their estates. I mean, what do they expect?

And to my delight, Mr. Miles was no exception.

Here's what I found out with just a touch of a button:

— Mr. Miles, AKA Christian Miles, is a fifty-seven-year-old real estate baron who was born in Nashville, Tennessee.

— He moved to Queens with his parents when he was seven years old, and this is where he developed the unique Southern/New Yorker accent that people associate with him.

— Christian Miles attended New York University, where he graduated with a degree in business and was a member of Alpha Omega Delta fraternity.

— After college, Miles took over his father's property management company, growing it from three apartment buildings in Queens to more than forty apartments, hotels, and businesses across New York City.

— He's been married twice but never had kids. His second divorce was especially messy, and his former Miss Delaware ex-wife settled for a cool $20 million, plus one of their vacation homes in the Hamptons.

— While he *does* own a penthouse overlooking Central Park, he spends most of his time on his lavish estate in Greenwich, Connecticut, which he bought for $30 million when he was just thirty-two years old.

— Though he's never come out and said how much he's actually worth, *Forbes* placed him at number 52 of the world's richest men.

— Christian Miles has a collection of expensive cars and stores them in a custom-built hangar with a revolving showroom floor and temperature-controlled environment. Allegedly, he's been known to race them down his half-mile-long private driveway during parties.

— Besides his car collection, he's also a collector of fine art, rare animals, and watches.

— The last big purchase he made was commissioning a personalized cell phone cover of his face.

— Rumor has it that Miles has a hidden vault somewhere on his 20,000-square-foot property where he keeps his rarest items as well as more than $1 million in cash.

And that was just what I was able to find out in the first ten minutes of my search. I would've gotten a lot more if I hadn't been interrupted.

"Fancy meeting you here," a voice said from behind me, jarring me out of research mode. I closed out of the search window as quickly as I could and swung around in my seat to see who it was.

"Ollie," I said, letting out a breath.

I silently cursed myself. I should've heard him coming up behind me. It's not like Ollie was exactly quiet. At the very least, I should've picked a computer station that allowed me to see people before they approached me. Who knows how many other kids had seen what I'd been doing?

Come on, Frankie! Rookie mistake.

"Doing some research?" Ollie asked, leaning against a nearby table and crossing his legs at the ankles. Today he was wearing a pair of black skinny jeans and a red-and-black-checkered jacket.

A big red bull's-eye would've made him stand out less.

"Nah," I said, trying to act as nonchalant as I could and hoping he hadn't seen what I'd been looking at before I'd shut it down. "Just killing time before class."

"Really?" Ollie asked, cocking his head to the side curiously. "'Cuz I thought maybe you were doing some recon work on your next mark."

Entry Eighteen

Wait—what?

I blinked as I wondered if I'd heard him right.

"What did you say?" I asked him slowly.

"Just that I thought maybe you were doing some research for your next job," Ollie said, shrugging. "That *is* why you were looking up Christian Miles, right? He's filthy rich. Loads to take there."

My head was swimming. I wasn't even sure where to begin processing what was coming out of Ollie's mouth. Did he know who I was? *How* did he know who I was? Did *everyone* know who I was? Was I really so out of my element here that I'd already totally given myself away? Was Ollie actually some evil genius mastermind sent here to thwart my every move?

"Not that I'm judging. I mean, if you *did* rob him, he'd totally deserve it," Ollie said when I still didn't respond. "The guy's the worst."

I closed my mouth, which had dropped open at some point during Ollie's speech.

What was I supposed to do now? Interrogate him? Couldn't exactly do that in a room full of kids. Threaten him? I didn't even know what he had on me yet, so that might be jumping the gun.

That meant I had to go with old trusty:

Deny, deny, deny.

"I don't know what you're talking about," I said, snatching my backpack off the desk and walking away from the evidence as quickly as I could.

I was betting on one of two things happening after this: either Ollie was going to follow me, in which case I could isolate him from the rest of the school's population and get all the info I wanted out of him without anyone else eavesdropping. Or he'd leave me alone and forget everything he'd seen.

I wasn't sure which I wanted to have happen more.

But after I slammed out of the library and into the crowded hallway, I heard someone behind me and knew Ollie had chosen door number one.

I headed straight for the nearest exit and took it, relieved to see that it led straight outside and to an area on the side of the school that was barely inhabited.

Nobody would bother us here.

"Hey, Frankie, wait up," Ollie called out as I continued to walk across the grass toward the soccer field.

When I was sure nobody was around, I turned abruptly and stalked back toward Ollie, who was clearly struggling to keep up with me.

"Who *are* you?" I asked finally, putting my face in his menacingly.

He took a small step backward. "Um, I'm . . . Ollie?" he answered, confused. "Don't you remember?

From yesterday? I was your welcoming—"

"Committee, yeah, I know that," I said, blowing past this. "I mean, who *are* you? How do you know . . . what you know?"

"Oh," Ollie said, realization registering on his face. "That."

"Yeah," I echoed. "*That.*"

"I've sort of known who you were since the first time I saw you," he said sheepishly. It was the first time I'd ever seen him look shy. He was usually so absurdly confident that it was weird seeing him this way and made me wonder if I'd underestimated him from the very beginning.

"How do you know who I am?" I asked slowly, my mind starting to whir with all the possibilities. Was he a spy recruited by the government to follow me and make sure I didn't continue my dad's legacy? Was he a rival thief trying to take me down?

"Uh, I'm sort of what you might call . . . an entertainment fanboy?" Ollie admitted finally, with a goofy smile.

This answer had not been anywhere on my list, and it showed on my face.

"A *what*?" I asked.

"An entertainment fanboy?" he repeated. "Like, I'm totally into all things entertainment and celebrity and infamy. Well, one of my biggest fascinations is true crime. It's really having its moment right now. I love to watch all that TruTV stuff and binged *Making a Murderer* and all those *E! True Hollywood Stories* of famous people who commit crimes . . ."

I started shaking my head like it might help make sense of what he was saying. When Ollie noticed this, he tried to get back on track.

"I was *obsessed* with your dad's trial!" he blurted out finally.

This revelation nearly threw me for a loop, but I forced myself to remain calm.

"I don't know what you're talking about," I said coolly, though I could feel myself starting to sweat.

Ollie raised an eyebrow at me. "Frankie, I *know* my true crime. And what your dad did was the crime of the century," he said, bluntly. When I didn't immediately confirm his suspicions, he sighed loudly and looked toward the sky. "They're not supposed to show kids in the news—for their privacy and safety and all—but I saw you. In the coverage. You were there every day. Sitting in the courtroom, watching it all happen."

I swallowed hard.

The gig is up, I thought.

"Look, your hair wasn't this boring brown color you've got going on now and the bangs are new—love them, by the way—but I *never* forget a face that's been on TV," he said matter-of-factly. "I knew who you were the minute I saw you, Frankie Lorde. What I've been trying to figure out is why you're *here*."

"My uncle lives here," I said, feeling like it was a safe enough response. I still wasn't admitting anything specific, but both of us knew he'd figured me out.

I began to walk away.

"Are you sure that's the *only* reason you're here?" Ollie pried.

"Pretty much," I answered.

"So, you're not here because, oh, I don't know . . . this is one of the richest places in the country?" he asked gleefully. "Plenty of people to rob and all."

I turned to look at him now.

"You don't know anything about me," I said stonily. "I'm just a kid, going to school in some stupid little town. Nothing more, nothing less."

"We both know you're more than that, Frankie," Ollie said quietly, closing the distance between us. "All I'm saying is . . . maybe we could help each other?"

I couldn't stop myself from busting out laughing.

"How could *you* possibly help *me*?" I asked.

"I can help you rob Christian Miles," he said at last. "And you can tell me all about your dad."

I looked at him blankly.

"Why do you want to know about my dad?" I asked.

"See, I'm an actor," Ollie explained quickly. "But I'm sure you could tell that. Anyways, all famous actors have had their big breakout roles. Brad Pitt had *A River Runs Through It*. For Julia Roberts, it was *Pretty Woman*. Zac

Efron had *High School Musical*. I really think your dad's story could be mine."

"Are you insane?" I asked bluntly. "My dad doesn't *have* a story."

"But he *will*," Ollie insisted. "And I want to play him when they make that movie. Or Netflix original."

"You *are* crazy," I said, shaking my head in disbelief and beginning to walk away.

"Look, Frankie," Ollie said, struggling to catch up to me. "All I'm saying is that I think your dad is wickedly awesome and I want to play him when I grow up. I mean, I think I could do him justice. You know . . . if I knew all there was to know about him."

I barely paused before answering.

"No way," I said.

"But I can help!" he called out. "With Christian Miles. I've lived here my whole life, Frankie. I know everything there is to know about this town. And I know *him*."

"*You* know a billionaire?" I asked, looking over my shoulder disbelievingly.

"Like I said, entertainment fanboy," he said, pointing to his chest.

"Still no," I said, and continued to walk.

"Don't you need a partner in crime, though?" Ollie asked loudly. "I mean, with your dad away and all? Who's gonna have your back?"

I cringed as he mentioned my dad being gone. It was enough to know every day that I was alone, but being reminded of it by a relative stranger? Not fun.

On the other hand, he wasn't completely wrong.

I've never done a job alone before. My dad has always been my partner. We've depended on each other. We've trusted each other more than anyone else in the world. And this trust has made every job we've done easier. There's been a sort of rhythm to it and we've both had our clear roles to play.

So how was I supposed to do this alone? In all the excitement of getting back in the game and going after Miles, I hadn't thought this part through.

Was Ollie right? Did I actually *need* a partner to pull this off?

And of all people, was the best person to do this Ollie? Crazy, over-the-top, stand-out-like-a-sore-thumb Ollie?

Then again, who else did I have around here who knew my big secret, had an odd infatuation with Dad and his work, *and* was willing to get into trouble with me if I gave the say-so?

I groaned and turned back around.

Ollie was already grinning at me, one hand on his hip like he was posing for someone.

"I'm not saying yes," I said adamantly.

"Okay," he said, nodding excitedly.

"Let's see if you can help me on the recon stuff and we'll go from there," I said, starting to walk away again.

"I can *totally* help with recon!" Ollie exclaimed. "I'm gonna be a great sidekick, Frankie. I promise."

"We're not superheroes, Ollie," I said. "More like villains, depending on who you ask."

I added the last part under my breath.

"Right," Ollie said.

Then he fell silent. For a second, I thought he'd finally left me alone. But then I heard him start to breathe heavily behind me as he caught up.

"But there are gonna be dope outfits, right?" he asked. "'Cuz I can totally do incognito fabulosity."

I dropped my head into my hands and sighed.

What am I getting myself into?

Entry Nineteen

"Who wants to go first?" Mr. Misaki asked, taking a seat on the edge of his desk and looking out at our class. When nobody jumped up to volunteer, he sighed. "Remember, extra-credit points to those who are willing to read part of their diary entries to the class. And there are more than a few of you who could use it."

At that, several reluctant hands went up around me.

"Great!" Mr. Misaki said cheerfully, and motioned for a messy-haired boy in the back of the class to join him in the front.

"I only have to read *some* of it, right?" the boy asked, looking and sounding nervous. "Not the whole thing?"

"Whatever part you think reflects what's going on in your world right now," Mr. Misaki said, as if this were an easy thing to do.

"Okay," the kid said, still sounding unsure. After shuffling through the papers in his hand, he finally stopped on a page and began to read aloud. "When I started writing my fan fic online, I had a total of two followers. And those were just other friends of mine who loved *Game of Thrones* as much as I did. But as I got more into writing the story about Dany stepping away from the whole war for the throne to open up her own dragon-breeding farm near Dragonstone, my numbers got crazy. Five thousand people have read my story so far and it's hard for me to keep up with the number of comments I'm getting. I'm even thinking of writing a sequel, bringing in a few of the other characters. The only problem is that I barely have time to write anything after doing all the homework I have for school. When I brought this up to my mom, she said homework comes first. But the way I look at it, people are enjoying my fan fiction more than my teachers are enjoying reading my homework, so . . ."

The guy looked up from what he was reading and sort of shrugged at Mr. Misaki, like he was expecting confirmation that this was true. After a second, our teacher realized this and sat up straighter.

"Oh, I don't know, Mr. Stanfield," Mr. Misaki said, clearing his throat and giving the boy a warm smile. "I'm quite enjoying your homework assignment right now."

"Well, yeah, because I'm talking about my fan fiction," the kid muttered under his breath before escaping back to his seat.

"Well done, Mr. Stanfield," Mr. Misaki said as he was once again left alone in the front. "I think it's a universal challenge to figure out how to devote equal time to your daily obligations and to your dreams and ambitions. Very relevant. Very relevant."

He nodded enthusiastically as he appeared to get lost in thought.

"Okay," he said, finally snapping out of it. "Next?"

Out of the corner of my eye, I watched Annabelle raise her hand beside me. I wouldn't have pegged her as someone who would voluntarily read her homework in front of the class—especially given how stupid she'd claimed the assignment was when it was first given—and I certainly couldn't imagine she would need the extra credit. She was so obviously a straight-A student. Or at least someone who wanted to seem like one. So I was surprised to see her practically skip up to the front of the class once Mr. Misaki had called on her.

She adjusted her paper in her hands and looked up from the words below as if she'd already memorized the whole thing.

"I can't sit idly by as other students at this school try to tear down the majestic legacy that those who have come before us have so dutifully worked to create," she said, sounding like she was delivering some grand political speech, rather than reading a personal diary entry.

My forehead wrinkled up as I tried to guess what atrocity she could possibly be talking about. A look around me showed that everyone else appeared to be just as much in the dark as I was.

"What I'm talking about, of course, is the state of *fashion* at this school. The clothing that a majority of the student body chooses to wear is simply atrocious. Girls mixing florals with stripes. Students shopping at"—Annabelle appeared to nearly gag before finishing her thought—"*Target*. Guys wearing clothes that were obviously meant for women—where will the madness end?"

As she mentioned her last point, Annabelle looked directly at Ollie. And because she was calling attention to him, the rest of the heads around the room turned too. Ollie just sat there, a blank look on his face, before slowly pulling his Burberry shawl tighter around his shoulders.

"By dressing this way, it's as if you are literally spitting in the face of every great person who has ever graced these hallways," she said, narrowing her eyes at him. "It's rude, and distracting, and the rest of us shouldn't be forced to see it. That's why I'm going to reach out to the student education board and propose we implement a mandatory dress code. Possibly even uniforms. The students at this school need to conform to the norm. Come on, people, be classy, not trashy."

Annabelle paused for dramatic effect as she finished, then looked over at Mr. Misaki as if for applause. He opened his mouth to comment but then closed it again. It was clear that he was just as confused and mystified by her speech as we were.

I looked over at Ollie, who had grown a little pink in the cheeks, and gave him a sympathetic look before rolling my eyes at Annabelle.

"Well, okay," Mr. Misaki said, trying to find the

words to follow that up. "You've given all of us a lot to think about, Annabelle. Thank you for sharing."

"Somebody has to stand up for what's right," Annabelle said before sauntering back to her seat and sitting down primly. Without looking straight at her, I could feel her turn her glare toward me like she was daring me to say something. Instead, I just trained my eyes on my own paper and waited for the bell to ring.

Entry Twenty

"You okay?" I asked Ollie when I saw him in the hallway later that day.

"Sure," he said nonchalantly. "Why wouldn't I be?"

"Well, there was that whole scene in Mr. Misaki's where Annabelle tried to assassinate your very being?" I offered quietly. "I just thought maybe it had bugged you. . . ."

"If I got bothered every time Annabelle said something stupid, I'd never have time for anything else," he said bluntly.

"So you're good?" I asked skeptically.

"Fan-freaking-tastic," Ollie responded, looking over at me with a forced smile on his face. "Okay, topic change. What's our next move? Do we need to trail Miles? I have a camera, I can take pictures."

Despite his possibly fragile state, I dragged him over to the side of the hallway where there were fewer ears listening.

"Dude, you need to *be cool,*" I whispered. "That means you don't advertise what we're doing to anyone who will listen. Got it?"

"Roger that," Ollie said, and did a little salute.

I rolled my eyes before beginning to walk again. I was headed to the cafeteria. For some reason I was starved today and the hodgepodge of smells wafting from the lunchroom actually smelled good. Visions of hamburgers and French fries and tacos and pizza danced through my head as I thought about all the things I wanted to stuff my face with. Ugh. How far I'd already fallen from my days of eating beef Wellington in the UK and osso buco in Italy. Just another reason attending school in the States was a dangerous idea.

"So where do we start, boss?" Ollie asked again, cutting into my thoughts about food. At least he wasn't yelling it across the school this time.

"Don't call me boss," I said. "And first we have lunch."

"Right," he said. "Gotta be fueled up before we go after White Tiger."

"What?" I asked, confused.

"I was just thinking, maybe we should give our target a code name. You know, so no one will know who we're talking about when we're talking about you-know-who," Ollie explained.

"And you chose *White Tiger*?" I asked, raising an eyebrow. "Because nobody will be curious about *that*."

"Well, then you choose," Ollie said. Then, a little sullenly, he added, "He does have a tiger, though. And it's a pretty cool code name."

"He owns a *tiger*?" I asked, surprised.

"Yeah," Ollie said. "At least, that's the rumor."

"Geez," I said as we joined the line of kids waiting to buy their lunches.

"We're not going to steal his tiger, are we?" Ollie asked me suddenly.

I gave him an are-you-kidding look. "We're not going to take his tiger," I confirmed. But even as I said it, I was thinking about how cool my dad would've thought the idea was. It was exactly the kind of job he would've loved.

But Dad wasn't here, and I was working with a novice as a partner, so stealing a freaking tiger wasn't going to happen.

"Oh, thank God." Ollie let out a nervous breath. "So what, then?"

I thought about this a minute, then shook my head. "Don't know yet," I answered honestly. "Gotta figure out what's most valuable. To him and to them."

"Them?" Ollie asked.

He was confused by this, and I realized it was a fair question. Ollie had no clue why I'd chosen Christian Miles as my target in the first place. I mean, yeah, the guy was loaded, and that was definitely part of it. But the real reason went deeper than that.

And if Ollie was going to put himself on the line for the job, he deserved to know why we were doing it.

"Do you know who my uncle is?" I asked Ollie.

"Sure," he answered. "He's a cop, right?"

I was impressed. Ollie had said he knew everyone in this town, and I was beginning to believe him.

"He's a detective, actually," I said. I'm not sure why I

corrected Ollie. He was close enough. "Anyway, he was working a case yesterday that didn't exactly go his way."

Ollie gave me a questioning look.

"Christian Miles manages these apartments over on the south side of town and he's been messing with the tenants who live there," I explained.

Ollie raised an eyebrow at me.

"Messing with them how?" he asked.

"Like, he's making them live in a dirt hole with rats and cockroaches and stuff, and refuses to make repairs. It's super disgusting and super shady."

"So he's a *slumlord millionaire*!" Ollie said, laughing at his own joke.

"Yeah," I said, holding back my laughter, even though deep down I sort of thought it was clever. "Anyway, when the people in the apartments fought back, he kicked them out or threatened to have them deported."

"What a creep," Ollie said.

"Exactly," I said.

"So I'm guessing Miles got away with it?" Ollie whispered.

"He's about to," I answered, pausing to order a cheeseburger and fries. "And it's not fair to all those people living there. They don't deserve to be treated that way. Especially since Miles has more than enough money to be a decent human being and is *choosing* not to. I mean, this is some evil dictatorship we're talking about. So if the system's not going to make it right . . ."

"Then we will," Ollie finished, placing his hands on his hips like Superman.

"Not superheroes," I reminded him.

"Okay, okay," he said, letting his arms drop to his sides.

After we'd grabbed our food, we began to look around for a place to sit. But before I could pinpoint the perfect eating spot, Ollie was nudging my arm, nearly making my drink slosh all over my lunch.

I gave him an annoyed look as I attempted to regain control over my tray.

"This way, partner," he said to me with a smile. "I think there's someone you should meet."

We weaved in and out of tables as Ollie led me over to one in the far corner. Just as we were about to pass the middle of the room, I saw a leg shoot into the walkway and managed to sidestep it just in time. I turned to look at the culprit, who was busy pulling her bootied foot back under the table she was sitting at.

"Sorry, Frankie, didn't see you walking there," Annabelle said sweetly to me.

The gaggle of friends surrounding Annabelle giggled as they watched the exchange.

"Right," I said slowly. And then, unable to help myself, I added, "I'd say we should get you some glasses, but I'm not sure you could pull them off."

Annabelle's friends let out a collective gasp as I turned around and continued on my way.

I didn't get why I'd become Annabelle's target in such a short time, but one thing was sure: I wasn't going to be an easy one. And as much as I'd prefer not to be noticed at all, no way was I going to be anyone's punching bag.

Dad didn't raise me that way.

By the time I caught up with Ollie, he had already arrived at a table that had four other kids sitting at it. There were three boys and one girl at different stages of eating, but they all stopped what they were doing as we approached.

"Hey, Ollie," one of the boys said, throwing out his fist and bumping it into Ollie's.

"Ryan!" Ollie answered, not waiting for an invitation to sit down.

"Man, James and I were just talking about when we're gonna have the next gathering of *Fortnite*! I can't wait to kick your butts again," Ryan said excitedly. "You're going down hard, son!"

I gave Ollie a sideways smirk as I sat down beside him.

"Uh, yeah," Ollie said, glancing at me, slightly embarrassed to be outed as a gaming nerd. "Definitely soon, bro. Hey, this is Frankie. Frankie, this is Ryan. He's a—"

"Fellow gamer?" I cut in, shoving a few fries into my mouth.

"You play too?" Ryan asked, looking at me like I was a magical unicorn he'd only ever read about in books. I guess girls around here aren't into gaming?

"A little," I answered. There'd actually been a six-month period when all my free time had been spent schooling online games. *Minecraft*, *Grand Theft Auto*, *Fortnite*—I played them all, only moving on to the next challenge once I'd mastered the previous one.

In the end, I realized nothing beats gaming people in real life.

"Really?" Ollie asked, surprised. He looked like he wanted to ask me more but then seemed to change his mind. "Frankie, Ryan lives on the south side."

"Oh!" I said, finally understanding why we were there.

"Why? You live there too?" Ryan asked skeptically as he took in my appearance.

"No," I said. "But I know someone who does."

"Ah" was all Ryan said to that.

"Maybe you know her? Her name's Estella Martinez?" I said nonchalantly.

Ryan chewed his food as he thought about the name for a bit. Finally his face lit up and he dropped the sandwich he'd been holding.

"Mrs. Martinez? Little old lady in Building 302?" he asked.

"Yeah," I said, though I had no idea where she'd lived. "That's her. Do you know her well?"

Ryan shook his head. "Just in passing," he answered. "But I haven't seen her around lately. I think she moved out or something."

"She's gone, but she didn't move out," I said. "She was kicked out by the landlord."

"That jerk?" Ryan said, a shadow crossing over his face.

"So you know him," I said.

"Seen him a few times, but never talked to him myself," Ryan said. "I just know he's given a few families trouble."

"But not you guys?" I asked, pushing the conversation a bit further.

"Nah. My dad's a handyman. We learned early on that anything that needs fixing, we have to do it ourselves. But we're lucky. Most of the other people who live there don't have that. They just have to deal with it. Either that, or"—Ryan put his fists up in the air and opened his hands like they were exploding—"poof. They're gone."

I nodded, knowing by now what he meant.

"So *that's* what happened to her," Ryan said, shaking his head. "You know, I always wondered. Then again, people come and go around there, so you never can tell."

"You know anyone else who's had problems with Christian Miles?" I asked him as I took a huge bite of my burger. Ollie gave me a funny glance as I felt a big glob of ketchup slide down the side of my mouth. Looking horrified, he handed me one of his napkins. I took it and wiped my face while simultaneously rolling my eyes.

The guy couldn't handle a real girl eating, how was he going to handle conning a billionaire?

"The better question is: Who *hasn't* had some sort of run-in with him?" Ryan said. "Like I said, he's a grade-A jerk. Always threatening someone about something. The only reason he leaves *us* alone is because we leave *him* alone. If we didn't, he'd try to get us deported in a second."

His eyes suddenly grew wide as he realized what he'd just said, and he glanced at me nervously. He'd obviously just remembered that I was a relative stranger to him and who knew if I was trustworthy.

"Not that we're illegal or anything," he said, backtracking, as he looked over at Ollie with concern.

"I didn't think you were," I said, not making a big deal of the comment. "Honestly, I couldn't care less if you were. None of my business."

Ryan looked relieved at this and visibly relaxed before diving back into his food.

"Why do you want to know about all that anyway?" he asked, cocking his head to the side as he studied me.

"Well, I know Mrs. Martinez and I just think it's really unfair what happened to her. I guess I wish there was something I could do to help," I explained, careful not to give too much away.

Ryan nodded. "That's cool of you," he said. "But I think short of giving everyone over there free room and board and fixing up all the things wrong with the dump, there's not a lot you can do."

"Right," I said, shrugging. "Figured I'd ask around anyway."

Ryan chewed for a few moments in silence, then pointed his sandwich at me as an afterthought.

"But if you ever decide to do something to get back at Christian Miles, I'm totally in for egging his house or something like that," he said, like this would somehow get back at the guy for everything he'd done.

"I'll let you know if I think of anything you can help with," I said, hoping this was enough to get Ryan to forget most of what I'd said before.

Because the plan that was beginning to form in my head involved way more than a trip to the dairy section at the grocery store.

Entry Twenty-One

"Why are we hanging out here?" Ollie asked, wrinkling his nose up in disgust. "It smells funny, and it's doing nothing for my complexion."

I paused in the middle of typing to take a deep breath. I'd found myself doing that a lot lately. It kept me from getting too annoyed and saying something I'd regret later. Because the truth was: Ollie was my only real ally at the moment. And although I hated to admit it—I think I actually *needed* him.

Besides, it wasn't like he was *all* that bad. I was simply used to having a partner I *didn't* have to explain every little thing to.

I bit my lip and wondered if Dad had ever felt this way about me. If he had, he'd never shown it. Which gave me even more motivation to try to be patient with Ollie.

"That's the smell of books and information," I said, pointing to the rows and rows of periodicals lining the walls of the room we were in. "It's a library. You're gonna have to get used to it if you stay in this business."

"But *why*?" Ollie whined. "Isn't that what the Internet is for? Looking up information in the comfort of your own home so you don't have to be around all these musty books and . . . dust? I can literally feel it clogging my pores as we sit here."

Breathe.

"Your pores are fine," I assured him. "And we're here because it's a public place with public access to the Internet."

"And . . . you don't have a computer at home?" Ollie said, fishing.

"Of course I do," I said. "I'm not a total weirdo."

Ollie made a sweeping motion with his hand at our current whereabouts as if he was questioning whether that was true.

"We're going to be searching for stuff we don't want people to know about," I explained. "More specifically, stuff we don't want the *government* to be able to trace back to us. Like, they would for sure be able to pinpoint that the research we're about to do came from this library. They could even tell which computer terminal we're using. But without photographic evidence or some sort of user info to prove we were the ones here, it'd be a dead end for detectives."

I paused here as I noticed the look of relief on Ollie's face. Seeing it, I realized I didn't want him to feel *too* comfortable about what we were about to do. That's how mistakes get made.

"Unless, of course, we were to do something while we're here that would draw unwanted attention to us, causing a witness to be able to describe us later, thus leading the trail back to us anyway. So I guess what I'm saying is, don't make a scene? Try to blend in, sink into the shadows. Be less . . . you. Anyway, the point is to do your research in public while being private about it. This is Thieving 101. Learn it, love it, live it."

"Ahhhh," Ollie said, the logic kicking in finally. "Big Brother. I got you."

He paused then and surveyed the room, in what I could tell was his way of being stealthy.

"Couldn't they be watching us right now, though?" he whispered, pulling the collar up on his red checkered jacket like it would suddenly make him invisible.

"They could be," I admitted. "But I scanned for cameras when we came in. They don't have surveillance set up anywhere. I guess stolen books isn't high on the list of this library's concerns."

"What about our phones? Can't they trace us through those?" he asked, sounding more and more paranoid by the minute.

"Why do you think I told you to turn yours off when we got off the bus?" I asked him, though I was more than a little impressed that he'd even thought to ask the question. Not many civilians think about all the ways the government can track its citizens. Even fewer take precautions to prevent it. Well, unless they have a need to.

Maybe Ollie wasn't completely hopeless at this stuff after all.

"Okay, so what's on the research docket today?" he asked after I'd been typing for a few minutes.

We were sitting at a cubicle in the corner, far away from most of the other patrons. This both ensured privacy so we could talk freely and guaranteed that fewer people would remember us being there.

Out of sight, out of mind.

"Right now, we need to get a comprehensive list of Christian Miles's assets," I said. "Any money he has in his possession, personal items that are valuable, anything that might be worth taking."

"Right," Ollie said. "Well, there's the tiger—"

"We're not stealing the tiger," I cut in forcefully.

"I *know* that," he said. "But you wanted a list of his assets and I was just starting out with the most obvious one."

He pulled a notebook out of his bag and opened it to a blank page. Poising the pen above the paper like an old-school secretary, he wrote what I assumed was *Tiger* at the top.

"What else?" he asked, ready to take down my notes.

"One article says he has more than a million dollars in a vault hidden on his property," I said. I paused as Ollie took his time sliding the pen across the page with a flowery flourish, then gave me a smile to indicate he was done.

"He owns more than twenty cars," I said next, reading an online feature published by *Architectural Digest*.

"Most of them are one of a kind and retail at more than a hundred K each."

"Yowza!" Ollie exclaimed. "I'd give up my signed copy of *A Star Is Born,* by Babs herself, to drive one of those."

"None of his art is listed by name, but it doesn't mean he doesn't have something valuable hidden away somewhere," I muttered. "He recently had a cell phone case commissioned of his own face from a famous jeweler, but I haven't been able to find its worth anywhere."

"I'd say that's stupid, but . . . ," Ollie said shyly, then held up his own cell phone, which was covered with what looked like a professional photo of him decked out in a purple paisley suit while posing against a glittery background.

I had no words to that, so I turned back to the computer screen.

"He also collects watches," I said, scrolling through an online photo album of Christian Miles's personal collection.

I didn't realize Ollie was peering over my shoulder until I felt his breath on my neck.

"Holy guacamole!" he said suddenly. "Who spends seventy thousand dollars on a watch? For that much, it better be able to freaking *stop* time!"

"Nope," I said. "Just tells it. But all fancy-like."

"What a stupid thing to spend your money on," Ollie said, shaking his head.

"And having twenty cars that just sit there is *practical*?" I challenged.

"At least they can take you places," he said.

"What you have to know is that rich people spend their money on a lot of stupid things," I said. "I've seen it so often that it doesn't even surprise me anymore."

"What's the stupidest thing you've seen someone buy?" Ollie asked, suddenly intrigued.

I had to think about this for a second. There had been so many. And what seemed stupid to me might not be all that stupid to someone else. Case in point, Ollie's obsession with cars.

"Um . . . can I choose two?" I asked finally.

"Sure," Ollie said.

"One guy we conned in England spent a small fortune on custom armored suits—for his *guinea pigs*," I said, remembering the tiny creatures wearing the heavy outfits.

"No way!" Ollie said, laughing.

"Yup," I said. "You should've heard the noise they made running around the chateau. You think hamster wheels keep people up at night? This was on a whole other level."

"Man," Ollie said. "Well, I can't imagine anything dumber than that."

"I have three words for you," I said, building the suspense with a big pause. "Gold. Toilet. Paper."

Ollie's mouth dropped open and remained there as he processed what I'd said.

"For real?" he asked when he'd finally regained his voice. "Like, dudes wipe their *butts* with it?"

"They might as well be using hundred-dollar bills every time they go to the bathroom," I said, smiling at the look on Ollie's face.

"Well, when you waste your money on things like that, don't you sort of deserve to be robbed?" he asked with a shake of his head.

"Totally," I agreed. "I like to think I'm doing them a favor. Like a cautionary tale, if you will. Buy stupid stuff, lose stupid stuff."

"You're saving them from themselves," Ollie put in. "In a way, you're actually a hero."

"I knew I liked you for a reason," I said, giving him a wink and letting out a little laugh.

We fell silent again as I continued to read through articles and features on Christian Miles. After ten more minutes, I pushed back my chair and stretched my arms over my head.

"I'll keep looking for stuff online, but I think we're better off just waiting until we're inside to see everything he's got," I said. "How does tomorrow look for you? After school, say around three? It'll give us enough time to look around before I have to be home."

Ollie blinked at me incredulously.

"You're talking *tomorrow* tomorrow?" he asked, sounding dazed.

I nodded like I didn't understand the confusion.

"As in, we go home, sleep, wake up, and it's tomorrow *tomorrow*?" he asked.

"Is there another definition of *tomorrow* that I'm not aware of?" I said to no one in particular.

Ollie sat down hard in a nearby chair.

"Isn't that like . . . fast?" he asked.

"No time like the present," I said. When I saw the frozen look on his face, I softened. "Look, you've been a big help so far, but you don't have to go any further with this. Not everyone's meant for this sort of thing."

"No," he said shakily, then sat up straighter in his seat. "I said I was in and I'm in. I just thought there'd be more . . . prep? Like, don't you need to teach me how to climb through windows and pick locks? Isn't there some crazy gymnastics routine I have to practice so I can get through the maze of infrared lights that will trip his alarms?"

Now it was my turn to look at him blankly.

"You want to learn gymnastics?" I asked, cocking my head to the side.

Ollie let out an exasperated sigh. "Well, aren't there tricks I need to be able to do to get to the gold? Like, all that ninja stuff they do in those *Ocean's Eleven* movies?"

"Can you do a backbend?" I asked slowly.

"No," he said.

"Then what makes you think you can learn gymnastics well enough to do some ninja routine?"

"I don't know!" Ollie exclaimed, throwing his hands

up in the air and causing the few people in the library to turn around and stare. "I just thought maybe I could *learn*."

"If you want to learn gymnastics, take a class. I think you could get PE credit for it at school," I said as an afterthought. "If you want to be a thief, you need to use the skills you already have."

Ollie paused as he took this in.

"But I don't have any skills," he said finally.

I gave him a sly smile as I walked over to him and placed my hand on his shoulder.

"Trust me, you have *just* the skills we need for tomorrow," I said, and clapped him hard on the back before walking away.

"Should I be scared?" Ollie called after me. When I didn't answer, he added, "I feel like I should be scared. Frankie? Frankie!"

Entry Twenty-Two

I love playing dress-up.

There, I said it.

Ever since I was a little girl, I've taken any chance I have to transform into someone else. It isn't because I didn't like being me. If I weren't me all the time already, I'd probably *want* to be me.

No. I like playing dress-up because it's exhilarating to step into someone else's shoes. When you put on a costume, you can do anything. Be anyone. A zookeeper. A princess. A witch with magical powers. A rich debutante. They're all at your fingertips as long as you have the right tools.

This is probably the one thing Ollie and I have in common. We're both natural-born performers.

Only, whereas Ollie's in it for the fame and attention, I'm in it for the thrill. There's something about taking on another personality, crafting a life that's so unlike your own that it stretches the limits of your imagination, that is the ultimate high. And who's to say that you aren't really Hilda, the Swedish exchange student visiting her aunt in the States for the first time? No one. Well, except for maybe your dad and partner, who knows that you're actually Frankie, the girl who doesn't even like eating Swedish meatballs and has only seen Sweden on a map.

134

But to the majority of the world at large, I can be Hilda if I want to.

That is, if the situation calls for a Swedish exchange student.

Becoming someone else—even for a short time—is one of the best parts about the job. I know it sounds crazy, but in a weird way, it's what makes me, me.

And I could tell it was the same for Ollie. That's why I knew he'd be perfect for phase one of my plan.

"So *this* is what a cop's house looks like," Ollie said after I'd pulled open our front door after school the next day.

"Detective," I corrected again, though I wasn't sure why. Maybe because I cringed a little anytime someone said the word *cop* now. Like it was a bad word or something. "And yeah. Is it everything you expected and more?"

"Eh," Ollie said, shrugging. "Not quite broody enough. And shouldn't we be in black-and-white?"

"I'll get right on that," I said, noting his reference to the old-school noir films. "In the meantime, I have something for you that you might like even better."

"Oh, goody!" Ollie said, clapping his hands together gleefully as he followed me up the stairs.

"Ta-dah!" I called out, and threw open my bedroom door grandly.

Ollie's grin slid from his face as he stepped inside slowly.

"Wow," he said with zero enthusiasm. "It's a girl's bedroom. However will I contain myself."

"This is where the magic happens," I explained, expecting a little more fanfare at the reveal.

Ollie raised his eyebrow at me skeptically.

"This is where phase one of our plan begins," I said with a smile. "Right here. In this room."

"Okay," Ollie said, sounding a little more interested than before but displaying none of the excitement I was feeling.

I quickly moved over to the bed and picked up the two outfits I'd laid out as soon as I'd gotten home. Without saying anything else, I turned around and held them up for him to see.

"Oh, wow. Okay," Ollie said after he'd had a chance to recover. "Gray isn't really my color—I tend to go for more . . . splashy shades? Fuchsia, turquoise, colors that have more than one syllable in them. And no offense, but I don't think *anyone* can pull off the jumpsuit look, except for maybe Queen Bey, but it was sweet of you to think of me—"

"These are our *disguises*," I said, cutting him off. "We're going into Miles's posing as high-end watch cleaners. These are our uniforms."

"Ohhhhhh," Ollie said, finally getting it. "So we're *supposed* to look drab!"

"Not drab," I countered, a little annoyed he was trying to chime in on anything involving the con. "The point is to fade into the background. Not stand out."

Ollie grabbed the jumpsuit out of my waiting hand

and looked at it with what could only be described as thinly veiled revulsion.

"Well, we certainly won't stand out in this," he said under his breath.

"Oh, calm down," I said, rolling my eyes. "You can change back into your ultrafab clothes when we're done."

"Are you sure this is going to be enough for them to believe we're professional watch cleaners?" Ollie said doubtfully. "No offense, but won't you just look like a kid dressing up in her mom's clothes?"

I gave him a look that told him I was offended.

"Not when I'm done getting ready," I said. "Remember, Ollie, this isn't *my* first time at the rodeo."

It was clear I was reminding him that *he* was the novice here. After that, he shut up.

"Now, I'm about to show you something that only one other person in the entire world has ever seen," I said, taking a few steps away from Ollie. I suddenly felt shy but forced myself to push forward through the awkwardness.

Ollie looked just as nervous as I felt, and he began to fidget with the material of his new uniform while training his eyes on the ground.

"You don't have to, really—" he began.

"This," I said, unlocking the bolts on my trunk, "is my thieves' tool kit."

Ollie raised his eyes slowly until they were trained on the now fully exposed red trunk in front of him. His eyes widened as he took a tentative step toward it.

"Oh!" he exclaimed as he saw what was stashed inside. He looked back at me as if asking for permission to go further. I nodded encouragingly.

Kneeling beside him on the floor, I began to take things out gingerly. There were dozens of wigs. Short blond ones. Long dark ones. Mousy brown ones. Every type of hairstyle a person could want. And they were high-quality, too. There's no point in wearing a disguise if people can tell it's a disguise.

Below the wigs was my makeup kit. It held everything from foundation, eye makeup, and lipstick to prosthetics and special molding clay to completely change a person's appearance.

There were bags of jewelry, some of it costume, while other pieces were real—and real expensive. Those, I'd picked up at different jobs along the way and only wore when the occasion called for it.

Tucked down at the bottom were outfits folded neatly and stored inside individual clear bags, each labeled with a code word so I could find it easily. But if I was being honest, I didn't really need the labels. As soon as I saw each bag I knew exactly what the outfit looked like and when I'd worn it.

It was rare that I'd wear a job outfit twice. This wasn't for the same reason that wealthy or famous people never repeat clothes. My reasoning was that each con was so unique it truly called for its own cover. But there was also the fact that memory is a funny thing. Almost anything can trigger a person's memory, and the last thing you want is for a shirt or dress to lead your mark back to you.

So outfits went into the vault, personas were finely crafted, and nothing was used that was a reflection of the *real* me.

Every thief has a tool kit and this was mine.

"What's in that?" Ollie asked when we'd reached the red-velvet-covered bottom, only to reveal an even more elaborate black box inside. It wasn't crude like a tackle box or something a handyman would keep. It also wasn't anything girly like a jewelry box. It was bigger than a bread box, black and sleek with different designs carved all over it. It managed to look both modern and ancient at the same time and it was one of my most prized possessions.

"This is my treasure box," I said, picking it up and holding it lovingly. "It's where I hide my most important things."

I slid a hand along the outside and felt its coolness against my fingertips.

"What kinds of things?" Ollie asked, sounding mesmerized.

I looked at him with mischief in my eyes.

"Wouldn't you like to know," I said, and placed it back in the bottom of the trunk.

Ollie opened his mouth in an objection, but I held up my hand to stop him.

"A thief has to have some secrets," I explained, like the conversation was over. "Now, let's get moving. We've got a job to do."

Entry Twenty-Three

Our transformation from middle school students to professional watch cleaners took all of forty-five minutes, but the result was drastic. After adding some wrinkles to both of our faces to age us a bit, we both chose wigs—mine was a black shoulder-length bob; Ollie went a few shades lighter with hair that grazed his shoulders. Accessories are key to rounding out any good costume, so I threw on a pair of oversized nerd glasses and a dainty nose ring, then tossed Ollie a hat that read TIME AFTER TIME.

Time After Time was the name of our fictional watch-cleaning company. Our logo consisted of the name superimposed on the face of a watch. I'd come up with the name myself but had created the logo using Photoshop and a stock image of an expensive watch I'd found online. Then I'd sent the logo over to a company at the mall that would place any logo or photo on just about anything you could think of.

Within an hour, I had Ollie's hat, a dozen fake business cards, and two patches that I affixed to our so-called *drab* gray uniforms—which were bought in cash, I might add, at a uniform supply store. They were originally meant to be hospital scrubs or janitorial staff gear, I think, but with a few minor changes, they'd become our watch cleaning company's uniform of choice.

All in all, it had been pretty easy.

Once we'd slipped on our jumpsuits, we stood in front of my floor-length mirror and admired our work.

"Not bad," I said, nodding.

"Are you kidding?" Ollie said. "We look like totally different people. I don't even think my mom would recognize me."

"I wouldn't go that far," I said, looking at him with a more critical eye.

There were things he'd need to learn if he was going to continue conning in the future. Like, changing his posture when he took on a different persona. Because the way he stood there—hand on his hip like he was constantly waiting for someone, chin tilted down so he could give you a bit of side-eye, tapping his toes to the sound of an unheard beat—was so utterly Ollie that it would be easy for anyone who knew him to figure out it was him underneath the wig and makeup.

I made a mental note to have him work on that later. When we didn't have a house to break into.

It took us a half hour to get out to Miles's estate—partly because he lived in an area of town called Back Country, which all the megamillionaires called home, and partly because we had to take public transportation to get there.

And the bus only went so far into the boonies before we found ourselves having to walk the rest of the way.

Which in our heavy jumpsuits and accompanying watch-cleaning gear proved more difficult than we'd expected.

"Tell me again why we couldn't just Uber?" Ollie asked, the sweat on his brow threatening to remove all the makeup I'd meticulously applied earlier.

"Duh," I said. "Do you really want to leave a detailed map of your whereabouts today, on one of the most-used apps in the world? I think not."

"Right," Ollie said with a sigh.

After a few more minutes, he groaned and said, "Please tell me we're almost there. I'm *begging* you."

"We're almost there," I answered automatically.

I would've said it even if it weren't true, just to get Ollie to stop complaining. But in this case, I wasn't lying.

Up ahead of us, I could see a tiny booth, the size of a shed, coming into view. It was like a mirage in the desert and at first I had to blink to make sure it wasn't going to disappear on me.

But a look at my burner phone—I'd grabbed two pre-paid cell phones at the mall when I'd picked up our other gear so that Ollie and I could stay in constant communication at Miles's house—confirmed we were indeed coming up on the home of Christian Miles, billionaire real estate mogul.

"Oh, thank God," Ollie let out as he practically gasped for air. "Do you have a Gatorade or something? A PowerBar? I think I need electrolytes. I feel like I just ran a marathon."

142

I rolled my eyes and handed him a water from my watch-cleaning bag.

"How about you let *me* do all the talking here?" I suggested. "You can be like . . . my *silent* partner. It'll be a part of your cover."

I waited for the pushback from Ollie, expecting him to complain about his lack of a speaking role in our plan, but he just nodded.

"Good," he said between breaths, "idea."

"Great," I said in a low voice as we got closer to the security gate. "Now, be *cool*."

"Cool," he puffed out. "Right."

"Can I help you?" a man asked as he stepped out from his spot inside the security booth.

The guy wore what looked like a perma-frown and immediately crossed his arms over his chest, forcing his muscles to protrude even farther from his body. The stance was meant to be intimidating, and I had to admit, it was working.

"Yeah," I said in a bored-sounding voice a few octaves below my own. "We're here to clean Mr. Miles's watches? We should be on the list."

The security guard raised his eyebrow, then slowly went back to his booth, returning with a clipboard of papers.

"And you are?" he asked.

I reached across my chest, pulled at the patch with our fake company logo on it, and pointed to the name stitched in black lettering underneath it.

"Time After Time?" the guy asked, with an unimpressed sound to his voice.

I wanted to say, *Well, let's see if you can come up with something better on such short notice*, but I kept my mouth shut as he ran his finger down the list.

"Sorry, don't have you on here," he said finally.

I'd expected this, since we had not, in fact, been added to any list allowing us entry to the house.

Ollie had no idea how I'd planned to gain entry to the estate, and as he watched the exchange, I began to feel his eyes boring into me. It took everything in me not to shoot him a look, but I didn't want to draw any more attention to him than he was already drawing to himself.

"Are you sure? How about under the name Val? That's me. Or maybe my boss, Bob? He's the one who set this whole thing up. Apparently, he thinks it would be a good idea to do this job pro bono, since Mr. Miles is a celebrity or something? That means free. Not that the guy can't afford it . . ."

I muttered this last bit like I was a slightly disgruntled employee who would rather be anywhere else, doing anything else than cleaning some dumb expensive watches at some billionaire's house.

The security guard, whose name tag read PHIL, sighed and scanned his list again. When he got to the bottom, he shook his head. "Nope. No Val. No Bob."

"Can you just call your boss? I'm sure it's just a mistake or something," I said. "Please? It's just that we're all the way out here already and if we go back to work without doing this, we'll just get yelled at and sent back another day. And then we'll have to bother you again. Just call him and see what he says?"

The security guard gave me a look that said calling his boss was the last thing he wanted to do, but I could also tell I was beginning to fully annoy him, and my ability to annoy seemed to win out.

He picked up his walkie-talkie and mumbled into it.

"Hey, it's me. The boss there?" he asked, just loudly enough for us to hear. "Yeah, so I got these guys from a company called Time After Time, that say he won some sort of free watch cleaning? They say their boss worked out the details? Yeah. It's free. Okay. Yeah. Yeah, bye."

The guard replaced his black walkie-talkie in its holder at his shoulder and went back to his booth. When he emerged, he walked over to Ollie and me and clipped VISITOR badges on our uniforms.

"Wait here," he said gruffly. "Someone's coming from the main house to drive you up and get you settled."

"Super," I said, matching his enthusiasm.

The guard opened up the gate and then went back into his booth, where he unceremoniously closed the door on us.

"What just happened?" Ollie asked in a whisper as soon as we were sure the guard couldn't hear us.

"I got us in," I said.

"But how did you know that would work?" he asked, looking both relieved and impressed at the same time.

"Something you need to know about rich people is that for all the money they have, they *really* love free stuff," I said. "It doesn't make any sense, I know. Then again, half the stuff they do doesn't make any sense. But it's true. If it's free, they can't say no."

Ollie just shook his head in disbelief.

As if out of nowhere, a golf cart suddenly appeared behind the large fence and came to a stop in the middle of the driveway. I had to squint in the sunlight to see who was behind the wheel but could just make out another muscly man, dressed in the same style of uniform as the guy in the booth. This one didn't have to cross his arms to make his muscles bulge out like a WWE champion. They just seemed to do it naturally. I wondered if Christian Miles found all his security detail at the same fitness gym.

"Come with me," the guy said, all seriousness and frowns.

It dawned on me then that the very large guard looked sort of funny sitting there in his tiny golf cart, and I had to hold back a giggle. It reminded me of a clown car; that much man just didn't quite fit into the vehicle he was driving.

Somehow I managed to hold it together and turned to Ollie to make sure he was following me.

That's when I saw that Ollie was having a tougher time keeping a straight face than I was. He looked one hundred percent freaked out. Like he was going to pass out any minute. So once we were seated in the backseat of the cart, I leaned toward him and gripped his leg firmly.

"Breathe," I reminded him, barely above a whisper.

I saw his chest begin to rise and fall at a slightly less hurried pace than before and finally let go of his leg. I took in the scenery as we made our way up the long, tree-lined driveway that led to Christian Miles's multi-million-dollar property.

It was much cooler under the cover of the trees than it had been out on the street, and I welcomed the breeze that blew across my overheated face and body. Luckily, I'd pinned the wig well enough that it didn't move an inch as we sped along, and the glasses kept the wind out of my eyes.

The air was quiet, like we were the only people for miles. The only things I could hear were the hum of the cart and its tires on the pavement and maybe the occasional bird chirping as we drove along.

I could see why Miles had paid an arm and a leg to live here. It was beyond peaceful.

And just as I'd gotten used to the peace and quiet, the trees suddenly opened up into a clearing that showcased a circular driveway and an enormous house looming behind it.

"Whoa," Ollie said under his breath as we drove up to the three-story structure that Christian Miles called home.

Entry Twenty-Four

If I hadn't been ready for it, I might've echoed Ollie's sentiment. But I'd done some research online before arriving and had seen dozens of pictures from an old posting of the house on a real estate website.

Still, nothing could've prepared me for seeing the house in all its grandeur, up close and in person.

Looking up at it from the cart was an intimidating experience. Miles Manor—as the plaque near the door read—was covered in gray stone and adorned with old-looking lanterns and gargoyles that peeked out over the edges of its roof. Ivy clung to the structure in places, giving it a slightly enchanted feeling. It sort of resembled an old castle, but with all the modern amenities expected of someone with wealth.

Two cars were parked outside in the sun. One I recognized as a Tesla; the other was a metallic-purple sports car. Both looked like they'd been brought out as decoration for guests who might stop by on a whim. Considering the guy had a garage full of them, it didn't surprise me that he might want to keep a few on display.

"Mr. Miles's house assistant will meet you inside to take you to the watches," the golf cart driver said, cutting into my thoughts and gesturing for us to vacate the vehicle and head toward the front door.

"Uh, sure," I said, regaining my voice. "Thanks."

I got out but quickly noticed that Ollie wasn't moving. He was still just staring up at the house.

"Um, *Stu?*" I said, using Ollie's cover name and hoping he'd remember it. When he didn't respond, I said it more loudly. "*Stu!* Move it."

I looked over at the security officer and made a face at him. "Sorry. He's new."

The security guy gave me a look that said he either understood or, more likely, didn't care.

I reached into the cart and practically pulled Ollie out of it. After stumbling a bit, he followed me to the door.

When we got there, I leaned in and rang the doorbell. I could hear the chime echo throughout the many rooms inside and cringed as I thought about how many people's days had just been interrupted.

Because no way did a house like this *not* have staff.

Seconds later, the door swung open and a round woman with bright pink cheeks peeked out at us.

"Well, hello," she said in the gentlest of voices. "I'm Mrs. Bailey. And you two are here about Master Miles's watches?"

Of course he would have his servants call him Master.

I disliked him a little more with every piece of information I learned about him.

I smiled at the woman in front of us and tried to tone down my disaffected youth persona, because she didn't deserve it. I was sure she got enough attitude from her employer.

"Yes, ma'am," I said politely, while still using the voice I'd created for Val. "If you can just point us in the right direction, we'll get out of your hair."

"Certainly," the older woman said, and stepped back to let us in.

Walking into Miles's foyer was like walking into another world. The entranceway could only be described as grand and was roughly the same size as the first floor of Uncle Scotty's house. There was a large round marble table in the center of the open space, which held the biggest centerpiece of flowers I'd ever seen, and the floors gleamed white and gold as the sunlight shone in through windows above us.

Beyond that were two sweeping staircases that started on opposites sides of the house but curved around and met in the middle at the second story. Beneath them was an opening that gave a clear view of an even larger room beyond it, with floor-to-ceiling crystal-clear windows. This was no doubt to showcase the incredible view of the backyard, which included an infinity pool, a rectangular pond at least two hundred feet long flanked by cobblestone walkways, several gardens, a tennis court, and a small concrete patch off in the distance that I recognized as a helicopter landing pad.

It was the epitome of luxury, and I knew from experience that the rest of the house would be just as impressive. Still, it wasn't my first time being in a house of this size, so the shock of it all wore off pretty quickly.

I held up my bag as a gesture that we were ready to get started and said to Mrs. Bailey, "Lead the way."

And lead she did. Up the stairs and through a labyrinth of hallways until we reached the end of one wing of the house, which turned out to be where Christian Miles's bedroom was. Mrs. Bailey pushed open the heavy double doors with little difficulty and then marched through the room and almost immediately into another adjoining room that was nearly as big.

That room turned out to be his closet.

It wasn't a normal closet, though. It was more like a small department store. Every available space was filled up with suits, button-downs, shoes, hats, and ties. Clothes were either displayed on silk-covered hangers or folded neatly on designated shelves.

The lighting inside had obviously been professionally done, spotlighting each section like a runway, and there was a triple-sided mirror at the end of the room to give Mr. Miles a 360-degree look at each outfit he tried on.

There was definitely no shabby dressing room effect in here. Only the best kind of perfection that money could pay for.

Mrs. Bailey walked over to a far set of drawers and pulled each one out one by one, displaying her boss's extensive collection of high-end watches.

As I ventured closer, I could see that each watch had its own space in a drawer, along with a gold placard describing the piece, the date Miles had gotten it, and its estimated worth. It was obnoxious, but I could at least appreciate the fact that he treated the possessions he collected with some sort of pride and respect. They weren't just bought to be tossed into a drawer somewhere. He actually *cared* about them.

And of course, this made me want to steal them from him. Because, well, it seemed like the Karmic thing to do.

"There you go," Mrs. Bailey said when she was finished pulling each drawer out for us. "I've disarmed the alarm so you can take them out of their places to clean them, and I'll check back in with you when you're done to make sure everything's where Master Miles likes it to be. Do you need anything before I take leave?"

"Do you have any—" Ollie began.

"No thanks. We're good," I said quickly, cutting him off and giving Mrs. Bailey an appreciative smile.

"Okay," she said, and began to walk away. "Well, give me a ring if you need anything."

She pointed to a button on the wall that appeared to be connected to an intercom.

"Thanks," I said, turning back to my bag and beginning to take out cleaning equipment. "We will."

As soon as she'd gone, I turned to look at Ollie, who was pouting in the corner.

"Rude" was all he said to me.

"If you ask for something, she comes back," I said bluntly. "Do you want her to come back or do you want to do what we came here to do?"

After a few moments, Ollie grumbled, "Fine."

"Okay," I said. "Good. Now, I'm going to start by looking around in the bedroom for anything that might resemble a hidden vault or safe or somewhere Miles might be stashing his more valuable stuff. Once I finish that, I'll head out to the other rooms of the house. I saw cameras around the whole estate—inside and outside—so I'm going to have to scramble them so no one finds out what we're really doing."

"And what should I do?" Ollie asked, looking at me eagerly for his assignment.

"You stay here and clean the watches," I said.

Ollie's face dropped.

"Are you serious?" he asked me. "We're really gonna clean them? *All* of them?"

"Look, we can't chance blowing our cover, and our slogan *is* 'Satisfaction Guaranteed,' after all," I said, holding in the slight bit of glee I was feeling. "Or *you* can be the one slinking around the house, trying not to get caught stealing from a billionaire. Either way. Be my guest."

We both knew there was really no choice there, and I waited for Ollie to accept it before going ahead with my original plan. Finally he huffed at me as he snatched the bag of cleaning equipment from the chaise lounge I'd set it on and turned his back.

"Fine. Whatever," he said miserably. "But I'm only giving it, like, seventy-five percent. I'm not giving it my all."

"Do what you've gotta do, Stu," I said before waving my fingers at him and heading out the door.

Entry Twenty-Five

Most people don't keep surveillance cameras in their bedrooms. Hidden cameras for their own personal use, maybe. But cameras that some security guy is going to be watching 24/7? Not so much. People are usually willing to give up a certain amount of privacy in their home for their safety to be guaranteed, but rarely will they give up *all* of it.

And from what I'd gathered about Christian Miles, he was the kind of guy who had secrets he wanted to keep hidden.

A quick glance around his bedroom proved my theory right, as there were no cameras to be seen.

So I got to work. I started by studying the walls. I looked for cracks or openings that could indicate there was something other than basic drywall there. I felt along the smooth wallpaper and knocked lightly in places to see if I could hear the familiar echo of an empty room on the other side. I pulled paintings and decorations away from their hanging spots to check behind them for safes or secret spaces or keys that would lead to treasures hidden somewhere else.

I looked under his bed, in between his mattresses, in the backs of his bedside tables. I riffled through the stack of books that had been strategically placed on a table-top near the lounge chair in the corner, just in case one of them was hollowed out and held something valuable within its pages.

There was nothing.

Well, nothing that was valuable enough for me to steal.

Which meant those valuable items were hidden some-where else on the property.

"Hey, I'm heading out to look around," I said to Ollie, popping my head around the corner of the closet door and startling him.

"Geez!" he said, bending down to pick up the watch he'd just dropped. "They should make you wear a bell."

"Now *that* would be a challenge," I said, nodding. "But I wasn't even trying to be quiet there. So keep an ear out here while you're in there. It'll be helpful for you to know if Mrs. Bailey is coming back. That way you're not caught off guard when she asks you where I am."

"What should I say if she does?" he asked, suddenly looking worried.

"Tell her I'm in the loo," I said. "She's not going to go in and see if you're telling the truth, and it'll give you time to get her to leave."

"Okay, but what if—" Ollie began again before I cut him off.

"You've done improv, right?" I asked him quickly.

"Sure," he said, his face going blank. "It's one of my specialties."

"Then just improv your butt off," I said. I gave him a big thumbs-up. "You'll do great, Ollie. I know you will."

Ollie's chest puffed up a little at the compliment and he went back to polishing the watch in his hands.

I took this as my opportunity to leave and ran lightly across the floor to the double doors, which Mrs. Bailey had closed behind her earlier. Pulling them open a few inches, I glanced out to survey the immediate area.

Nobody was in the hallway as far as I could see, and there were only two cameras visible—one directly across from the bedroom door I was currently peeking out of, and the other at the end of the hallway. More specifically, the exact direction I wanted to go in to search the rest of the house.

Slipping back inside the bedroom, I pulled at the snaps on my jumpsuit until they sprang open like those rip-away pants basketball players wear. The only difference was that the lining of my uniform held all the tools I needed to move through any place undetected.

I pulled a small black rectangular object out of its hiding place near my armpit. It looked a lot like the walkie-talkie the gate guard had used earlier. Only, this one had three antennas sticking out of the top and was definitely not a walkie-talkie. This was a scrambler. One that could wirelessly disable any surveillance camera within twenty feet of it.

It was a gift from Dad for my tenth birthday. He'd also bought me an American Girl doll, which I'd immediately renamed Marm after Fredericka Mandelbaum, a famous Prussian-born con woman who owned her own thieves' den in New York in the 1870s.

Eventually I grew too old for Marm. But I never outgrew the scrambler.

I pressed the button on the little black box, watched as the light on top shone blue, indicating that it was working, and then shoved it back inside my jumpsuit. Then, with a deep breath, I slipped out of Christian Miles's bedroom.

As I made my way down the long hallway, I ran my hands over the walls, checking for possible hiding spots as I went. I didn't actually expect to find anything there—the area was much too out in the open for there to be an entrance to a secret room. Miles would've wanted at least a little seclusion if he planned to be slipping in and out of a room he didn't want anyone else to know was there.

And a main hallway like this just wasn't conducive to that.

So I quickly moved on from one room to the next until I was satisfied that every inch of the upstairs had been thoroughly checked.

This was no small feat, given the massive size of the house, and when I was finished, a look at my phone told me I'd already burned through forty-five minutes of my time in Miles's house.

It wouldn't be long before Mrs. Bailey came back

158

to check on us. I was sure of that. And it was in our best interest for me to be back there with Ollie when she did.

But I also knew we wouldn't have another chance at unfettered access to the house like this again. Well, not before the actual break-in.

I shot down a back staircase as quickly as I could while still being quiet and wandered into the first room I came to.

It turned out to be Miles's office. Or library. Or man cave. Or maybe it was meant to be a combo of all three. Either way, rows of books lined three of the walls, and the built-in shelves holding them extended approximately fifteen feet to the ceiling.

As I moved farther inside, I could just make out particles of dust as they swirled around in the air, only visible because of the light shining in from outside. Directly in front of the large bay window sat an oversized mahogany desk with intricate designs winding their way up the legs and then disappearing into the smooth surface of the top as if they'd never been there in the first place.

The desk itself was a piece of art, and it made sense that there were no framed pictures in the room.

Now *this* was the kind of place where a person would build a hidden room.

I started in one corner and began to pull on the book-shelves in different places, expecting each time that some-thing would give way and the whole wall would open up for me. But nothing moved, even when I threw all my weight behind my efforts.

Breathing heavily from the physical exertion, I started again, this time getting down on all fours and putting my face up against the space where the shelves met the floor. If there was a secret room behind these bookshelves, I'd likely be able to feel the air escaping and at least be able to pinpoint where it was.

As I was crawling behind Miles's desk to make my way to the other side of the room and continue my search, I heard footsteps in the hallway. With barely enough time to dive out of sight, I pulled myself into the narrow space between Miles's leather chair and his desk and hid.

Seconds later, the door opened and people walked in.

"Braxton wants to know how much security you want for the fifteenth," a deep voice said as the footsteps made their way farther into the room.

Two sets of footsteps, I noted.

"How many people are supposed to be here?" another voice asked. This one had a slight southern drawl mixed with a hint of something tougher.

Christian Miles.

"Roughly two hundred," the first voice answered. It didn't take a detective to guess he was a part of Miles's security detail. Maybe even the head of security. "I'd suggest having at least twenty men. Ten visible and ten behind the scenes."

"Very well," Miles answered, not thinking about it long.

The security guy continued. "There haven't been any threats connected to the event, and—"

"I said fine." Miles cut him off.

"Yes, sir," the man responded.

"Anything else?" Miles asked, sounding distracted.

"A few of the cameras around the property seem to be acting up again, but I have our tech guy on the way to check it out," the man said. "I don't think it's anything to worry about. And I'll make sure everything's working again by the fifteenth."

"Good, good," Miles murmured before switching topics. "I'm heading into the city in ten and will need a few people to come with me. Send them out to the heli in five."

"Yes, sir."

"Oh, and don't give me the squirrelly guy, the one with the glasses?" Miles added with a hint of a sneer in his voice. "He always turns green when we hit turbulence and I don't want to smell like vomit when I meet with the Parkerson Group."

"Of course, sir," the man said. "I'll send Harper and Voight."

"Fine" was all Miles said before one of the pairs of footsteps retreated from the room and then disappeared altogether.

At this point, I was alone in the room with only one other person. And there was no way for me to tell if that other person was Miles or his security detail. Not that it mattered. I *so* didn't want to run into either of them.

So I waited.

Until finally, after a few more minutes of silence, the person began to move again, this time making his way across the room.

And right toward me.

I froze in my spot under the desk and tried my best not to breathe. If he came to sit down, it would all be over. Because there would be no excuse for a watch cleaner to be hiding in a billionaire's personal office/library/man cave that would possibly fool anyone.

Please don't come over here. Please don't come over here.

Not that this was the first time I'd found myself in a tight situation. I mean, every heist or con seems to derail in one way or another. The difference was, I'd never had to clean up the mess on my own before. Dad had always been there to either think fast or have my back if things went awry. So this was sort of new territory for me.

I'm not one to pray, but what the heck. It didn't hurt to throw it out there.

And then I heard the person stop a few feet away from where I was hiding and pick something up. Something that made a distinct clinking sound as it hit his ring or watch. There were two more loud clinks and then the sound of liquid being poured into a glass.

Whoever it was had gone over to the bar that was set

up in the corner and was helping himself to a drink. I could hear him gulp it down and pour another. The pungent smell of liquor filled the air and I wrinkled up my nose in disgust. It smelled stale. And funky. Like whatever he was drinking had gone bad.

Then again, most alcohol smells bad to me.

After the person had downed his second drink, he replaced the empty glass and followed the first pair of footsteps out the door, letting it slam shut behind him.

When I was sure I was alone again, I finally let out the breath I'd been holding in.

I had to get out of there. And fast.

The security guard had said the surveillance cameras weren't working properly and someone was on their way to check it out. That meant that someone would be going into Miles's bedroom soon and would find one of the watch cleaners was not actually where she was supposed to be—cleaning watches.

I pushed the chair away from the desk and bent forward to crawl out, but paused halfway.

And then looked down at the floor beneath my hands.

I hadn't noticed it while I'd been hiding. Maybe because I was too focused on what Miles and the security guy were saying, or too freaked that I might get caught. Either way, I couldn't believe I'd almost missed it completely.

But now I was in the perfect position to stumble on what I'd been looking for all along. I traced my finger along the line that ran across the floorboard behind the desk. You wouldn't even have noticed the crack unless you were looking for it.

Or, like me, you felt air coming from down below.

It *had* to be Miles's secret room.

And I'd found it.

Entry Twenty-Six

Now I just had to figure out how to get in.

I began rummaging around on the floor, pulling at any cracks I could find, thinking maybe there was a hidden panel beneath the desk that opened to some sort of keypad or lock. But that turned out to be a bust.

So I began to search through Miles's desk. I looked inside every drawer, practically emptying them out, hoping to find the lock that would gain me entry. But again, there was nothing.

How the heck was I supposed to get in there?

I collapsed back into Miles's chair, noticing almost instantly how comfortable it was. I rocked back and forth a few times as I racked my brain to figure out where the keypad might be hidden. It had to be easily accessible to him. No way would a guy like that be willing to jump through hoops to get to his own treasure room.

No, it *had* to be nearby.

I glanced around absently at the things on Miles's desk as I rocked back and forth. Finally my eyes fell on an iridescent envelope peeking out from a pile of papers on the corner. Pulling it free, I slid the card all the way out and read through the details that were printed across it in glittery script.

My excitement began to grow as I slowly traced my fingers along the raised writing. As I came upon the last letter, I tapped the card on the desk happily, placed it back in its envelope, and hid the whole thing inside the pocket of my jumpsuit.

Leaning back in the chair once more, I redirected my attention to Miles's hidden treasure room. My time to gain entry was quickly running out, and while I had the where, I still hadn't figured out the how.

What I *did* notice was that in all my rocking, I'd moved the chair a few feet away from the desk. With a sigh, I leaned forward to grip the edge of the desk and pulled myself back again.

That's when one of my fingers slid across something on the underside of the desk. Something that shouldn't have been there. Something round and buttonlike.

As I pushed it, I let a smile grow across my face.

A small whooshing sound cut through the air and I watched with widening eyes as the top of the desk began to separate in the middle, revealing a small control panel the size of a book.

It contained just a speaker and a black square of glass.

"*That's* what I'm talking about," I whispered, glancing back up at the door to the room as if someone might walk through it any minute.

"Prepare voice recognition and fingerprint scan," a computerized woman's voice said with a British accent.

I wondered if Miles had had his choice of accents when

it came to his computerized security, and then I speculated on why he'd chosen a British one. He was famously known for not particularly liking countries other than his own, so it was curious that he'd want a British-sounding voice talking to him every day.

"Voice recognition and fingerprint scan about to commence," the same voice said, this time a red line appearing and lighting up the black glass above it.

Without hesitating, I pushed the button underneath the desk again and watched as the whole table closed back up, concealing what was hidden within.

I glanced back down at my watch and shot up out of the chair.

I had everything I needed, and now I had to get moving.

Placing everything back where it had been, I raced across the room and listened at the door before sneaking out and back up the stairs. I didn't run into anyone. If I had, I could've just said I was looking for Mrs. Bailey and had gotten turned around. It would've been a plausible excuse, but not having to make one in the first place was even better.

One of the double doors to Miles's bedroom was slightly ajar as I tiptoed up to it, and I paused midstep before going in. I had definitely closed the doors all the way before going on my search around the house. So either Ollie had opened the door at some point while I was gone or . . .

"And then we just take this little brush here—it's

actually called a bushy prickle, just a fun little fact there—and I run it across the sides here with the organic adamantium solution I was telling you about earlier, and it disintegrates any subatomic particles that might have adhered themselves to the surface."

I could tell at once that it was Ollie who was doing the talking, but I had no idea what he was talking about.

As he rambled on, I snuck across the room and into the bathroom, flushed the toilet, and threw my hands under the faucet for a few seconds before heading straight for the closet where I'd left Ollie an hour before.

"Sorry about that," I said, breezing into the room like I'd never left. I faked surprise at seeing Mrs. Bailey standing there next to Ollie, who was holding up one of the watches for her to see.

I cast my eyes down at the floor like I'd just been caught.

"Bathroom break," I explained, trying to look embarrassed. "Sorry, I wasn't sure where the guest bathroom was . . ."

"Not at all, dear," Mrs. Bailey said, so thoroughly enthralled with what Ollie was saying that it was as if she'd forgotten I was supposed to be there at all. "Stu was just telling me all about your fantastic company and how you get these watches so clean. I was hoping to get a few pointers for when Master Miles wants me to polish them up between cleanings."

"But—but as I was explaining, it—it's our company's patented cleaning solution that really makes the difference," Ollie said, stammering slightly as he tried to bring me up to speed on the lies he'd been telling Mrs. Bailey.

"You didn't tell her about the *organic adamantium solution,* did you?" I asked, trying to sound alarmed even as I raised an eyebrow at him.

Mrs. Bailey was still staring at me, so she didn't see Ollie blush bright red.

"Oh, I'm afraid he did," Mrs. Bailey said, looking like she'd just gotten her new friend into trouble.

"Stu, you know that's a company secret," I scolded lightly. "If Bob were to find out—"

"Oh, dear, I promise I won't say a word," Mrs. Bailey insisted earnestly.

I could tell she meant it. I almost felt bad about lying to such a sweet lady, but we needed to get out of there without suspicion. And soon. Before the security team came looking for the reason that the cameras had been acting up.

Namely, me.

"Okay," I said, making it seem like I still wasn't sure. Finally I just waved my hands in the air like I'd given up. "Well, I guess what Bob doesn't know won't hurt him, right?"

Ollie had already begun to place the watches back in their designated spots in the drawers, and I walked over to pack up the bag.

"Well, we're all finished here, Mrs. Bailey," I said, zipping up the cleaning tools and heaving the whole thing over my shoulder. "No need to see us out."

Ollie and I began to walk away and had already made it halfway across Miles's bedroom when Mrs. Bailey's voice suddenly called out behind us.

"Wait right there," she said, the words coming out like a command.

We both stopped cold in our tracks, and I closed my eyes while taking a deep breath.

Had she somehow figured out we weren't who we said we were? Did she know that I'd snuck out of the room and had been gone for over an hour? Were we about to be caught?

I turned around slowly, prepared for the worst, and caught the look on Ollie's face.

It was pure terror.

"Yes?" I asked, forcing my voice to come out calm and even.

Mrs. Bailey walked over to me and stopped just a foot away, holding out her hand expectantly.

"Your business card?" she asked finally. "I'd like to pass it along to Master Miles and tell him what a wonderful job you did. After he sees the work, I imagine we'll be having you back around."

I let out a breath but hid it behind a warm smile. Then I slid my hand into one of the many pockets of my uniform and presented her with a card.

"Thanks so much, Mrs. Bailey," I said, already feeling guilty that if all went as planned, she'd never see us again.

Entry Twenty-Seven

"A *bushy prickle*?" I asked before bursting out laughing. "*Organic adamantium solution*? Now remind me, do we get ours straight from outer space or is that shipped through Amazon?"

We were back on the bus headed home, having managed to make it off Miles's property without encountering any other issues. I hadn't had a chance to tell Ollie everything I'd learned while traipsing around the house, since I'd been too busy making fun of the little story he'd told Mrs. Bailey.

"Go ahead and laugh, but she bought it, didn't she?" he said, folding his arms over his chest.

"But *adamantium*?" I asked, shaking my head at him.

"It was all I could think of," he said, shrugging.

"You better hope her grandkids aren't fans of *X-Men*," I said, my laughter dying down to a chuckle.

"Well, feel free to come up with the lies yourself next time," he said, scowling. "I was only trying to save *your* butt, remember?"

"You're right, Ollie. My bad," I said, forcing the smile from my face. "You really *did* do a good job back there. She didn't suspect anything."

He gave me a bit of side-eye before seeming to forgive me.

"Thanks," he said finally. "Yeah, it sort of came naturally. You know, because of the improv stuff."

I nodded like this totally made sense.

"So what did *you* discover while you were off sneaking around?" he asked.

I brightened.

"I found it, Ollie," I said, excited to share the details with him.

This feeling actually caught me by surprise. When I'd agreed to let Ollie join me on the job, I thought he'd mostly get in the way or be a liability. But I was beginning to realize that part of the fun of a con was working *with* someone while doing it. It was reveling in the excitement of coming up with a plan and then being able to celebrate with someone when you were victorious.

It was a part of the whole experience that I'd never known was vital.

Before now.

"Found what, exactly?" Ollie asked, mirroring my excitement. Then he suddenly looked worried. "Not the tiger, right?"

"No, not the tiger," I said, brushing that off. "I found *it*. Miles's secret treasure room."

"And?" Ollie asked, bouncing up and down in his seat a little. "What kind of treasure are we talking about? Art? Rare Egyptian figurines? Diamonds and rubies?"

"No clue," I said, just as excitedly as if I'd said yes to all the above.

Ollie's face dropped.

"I don't get it," he said.

"You need voice recognition and a fingerprint scan to get into the vault, and obviously I didn't have those on me when I found the room, but that doesn't really matter. And neither does *what's* inside," I explained quickly. "The point is, *I found it!* There's a hidden room where a billionaire stores his most valuable stuff and *I found it.* Can't steal something you can't find. Get it?"

Ollie nodded slowly like he was humoring me.

"Okay," he said. "So we *know* we're going to steal something, we just don't know *what* we'll be stealing yet."

"Right," I said.

"But we know where it's hidden," Ollie continued. "So we're . . . good?"

"Yep!" I said, smiling.

"And we'll be breaking in there . . . soon?" he asked.

"That's the best part," I said, reaching inside my jumpsuit and pulling out the envelope I'd stolen off Miles's desk.

I handed it over to Ollie and watched him take out the contents and scan them.

"'You are cordially invited to the Miles Masquerade Gala to benefit the National Constitution Center,'" Ollie read out loud. "'Please join us at Miles Manor on the Fifteenth of September, for drinks, dinner, dancing, and a live auction to benefit the NCC. Dress in your best masquerade ensemble. RSVP. Please present your invitation at the door.'"

Ollie looked up from the invite and blinked at me.

"We're crashing a gala?" he asked.

"It's not *crashing*," I argued, grabbing the card from his hand and waving it in front of his face. "We have an invitation. See?"

"In a week," he said, sounding awestruck.

"No time—" I started.

"Like the present," he finished, shaking his head at me.

"See? You're a natural at this, Ollie," I said, clapping him on the back jovially. "Now all we need to do is get our covers together, do some digging into Miles's financials, work out a plan that will get us both his voice ID and fingerprint, brush up on my pickpocketing skills, prep you for the performance of a lifetime, and pretty much plot out the largest heist this town's ever seen. All while going to school and making sure my uncle never finds out."

Ollie let out a laugh that sounded on the verge of hysterics.

"Easy peasy," he said before slumping back into his seat dramatically.

Entry Twenty-Eight

"I had no idea you liked Indian food," Uncle Scotty said, skeptically studying the bowls of food that had just been placed in front of us.

It was my night to choose where we ate dinner and I'd been craving something spicy. So I'd fallen back on an old favorite. Sure, we'd had to travel a little farther than usual for takeout, but it was worth it.

At least as far as I was concerned. I wasn't so sure Uncle Scotty felt the same way. In fact, he still hadn't tried any of the dishes I'd ordered for us. Just kept staring at them like they might turn into something he recognized, like pizza or burgers or even a salad.

I held back a giggle as I watched him battle with his desire to be a good sport and his fear of anything that might bring him out of his comfort zone a little.

"Oh, yeah," I said, grabbing a piece of naan from the middle of the table and dipping it into a bowl of chicken vindaloo. Popping it into my mouth, I savored all the flavors. There was nothing like it. "There was one point where Dad and I ate Indian for a whole month straight. He complained about heartburn after every meal but kept going back for more."

"What's that green stuff?" Uncle Scotty asked, pointing to one of the bowls.

"That's palak paneer," I said, dipping another piece of the Indian bread into the dish he was pointing at. "It's like—spinach and cheese. It's really good. Here, try some!"

I held out a piece of the bread smeared in the sauce and a little chunk of cheese. He just shook his head vigorously and sank back into his chair as far as he could.

"No thanks," he choked out, making a face. "It looks like what comes out of a babies' diaper."

"Tastes like it too," I said, shoving the whole thing into my mouth. When I saw Uncle Scotty's horrified look, I laughed. "I'm kidding. You have no idea what you're missing."

"That's okay," he said, scooping up some of the plain rice and putting it onto his plate instead. "I don't mind being left in the dark there."

I chuckled and continued to fill my plate.

"So how's the case going?" I asked him once I came up for air.

"Ruling came in last night," he said, tasting the rice gingerly. "They found in favor of the defendant."

"*Of course* they did," I said without hesitation.

"I really thought maybe we had this one," Uncle Scotty answered thoughtfully. "I mean, I know *you* said you had it all figured out, but I was still hoping . . . I don't know."

"That they would do the right thing?" I finished, understanding what he was feeling. "Yeah. I wish I'd been wrong."

Uncle Scotty gave me a look.

"I'm still not convinced it all happened the way you say it did," he said. "The judge being in Christian Miles's pocket seems like a bit of a stretch to me. But yeah, I wish you'd been wrong too."

"I *do* think you were right about something, Uncle Scotty," I said, mouth full.

"You do?" he asked, sounding surprised. "What's that?"

"I'm starting to come around to your way of thinking about Karma and all that," I said. "I have a feeling that one way or another, Christian Miles is going to get what's coming to him."

Uncle Scotty gave me a funny look and continued to study me as I stuffed my face. It looked like he was about to ask me what I meant by the comment, so I changed the subject as quickly as I could.

"I think I made a friend at school," I blurted out, hating how needy it sounded. I didn't want Uncle Scotty thinking I had been longing for a friend or anything. But I also knew that making friends was a step that would make him think I was thriving and moving on with my life. And I knew it would distract him from our previous conversation.

"Really?" he said, his eyebrows shooting up.

"Don't sound so shocked," I said. "I can make friends."

"I'm not shocked you found someone who wants to hang out with you," Uncle Scotty said, taking another bite of his rice. "I *am* surprised there's someone who meets *your* standards."

"He doesn't," I said. It was a knee-jerk response, though. And not totally true. "I mean, he's okay. He's not as bad as everyone else."

"Your friend's a *he*?" Uncle Scotty asked, his brow furrowing.

"Gross," I said, dismissing what he was implying. "It's not like that. Ollie's just a friend. He's like having a girlfriend around."

"Okay," Uncle Scotty said slowly. He was silent for a bit, seeming to mull this over. Finally he cleared his throat and continued, "Frankie, did your dad ever have the talk—"

"Oh, God, no, stop," I said, dropping my fork with a clang and throwing my hands over my ears. "Would it help if you met him? You'll see how *so* not-needed this conversation is."

"Yeah," Uncle Scotty said, still looking uncomfortable about the whole thing but appearing satisfied for the moment by the offer. "I think it would be good for me to meet your new *friend*."

"Ollie," I reminded him.

"Ollie," he repeated.

"Done," I said, hoping we were all finished with that.

178

After a few more moments of uncomfortable silence, Uncle Scotty continued.

"So the other kids are awful, huh?" he asked.

I held back the sigh I was feeling. I'd forgotten for a second that Uncle Scotty was a detective and he didn't miss much. Meaning, he hadn't glossed over the comment about the rest of the student body like I'd hoped. He'd simply filed it away for a later discussion.

Which appeared to be happening now.

"Not all of them, I guess," I said, trying not to grumble. "There's just this one girl and her minions who don't seem to like me much."

"Any reason why?" he asked.

I raised my eyebrow at him.

"Are you asking if I did something to piss them off?" I said.

"Language," Uncle Scotty reminded me. "And . . . well, yeah. Did you?"

I gave him one of my biggest eye rolls ever, just to be sure he knew how silly I thought the question was.

"No," I said finally. "The teacher made this girl, Annabelle, share her book with me in class. After that, she sent me the wrong way to class and then tried to trip me at lunch."

"Maybe they were just accidents," he suggested.

I shook my head. "She knew exactly what she was doing," I said. "She's just, you know, annoying."

"How is she to the other kids in your class?" he asked.

"Equally awful," I said. "I mean, I seem to be her focus right now, but Ollie said she's just like that."

"Does she target Ollie, too?" he asked.

"Yeah," I said, thinking about Annabelle's jab at him in class. "Not that he'd admit it, though."

"Do you want me to talk to the school about it?" Uncle Scotty asked.

"Nah," I said, waving him off. "I can handle it."

"Not with your fists, I hope," he said, looking worried again.

I shot him a look. "Not my style," I said. "I'll just ignore her and she'll get tired of it all. No need for me to stand up or stand out."

I didn't add that the last thing I wanted was for Annabelle and her clones to know I was a threat. I wanted to remain a nonissue. At least for as long as it could be beneficial to me.

"There might come a time when you need to stand up, though," Uncle Scotty said, cutting into my thoughts. "I know *you're* strong. I know *you're* fully capable of taking care of yourself. But not everyone can. So while I'm not saying you should go out there and kick bully butt, if you have a chance to stand up for someone who can't stand up for themselves, I hope you'll take it. Because there's nothing more noble than standing up for what's right."

"Okay, Captain America," I said sarcastically, even though I knew he was being serious.

It was sort of sweet, though, in a way. You could tell

he was trying to remind me that I could join Team Hero instead of Team Career Criminal. That I was capable of doing some real good.

Too bad he was going to have to settle for something in between the two.

Entry Twenty-Nine

"Your uncle wants to meet me?" Ollie asked the next day at school. "Am I in trouble or something? I mean, in the movies it's never a good sign when a detective wants to talk to you."

We'd been walking around the school grounds after lunch, when I'd remembered Uncle Scotty's invite. Or request, rather.

"You're not in trouble," I said, rolling my eyes. Then I paused. "What do you think you'd be in trouble for anyway?"

Ollie took a beat to think about this.

"My killer fashion sense?" he said finally.

As if to prove his point, he ran a few feet ahead of me and then turned around and walked back toward me like he was on the runway at a fashion show. Today he was wearing a long black-and-white-striped jacket that appeared to be a cross between something from *Sherlock Holmes* and *The Devil Wears Prada,* and all white underneath. With each step, the jacket billowed behind him dramatically like a cape.

Other kids started to turn and watch Ollie prance toward me. Some let out whistles, cheering him on, while others stared and whispered. I wanted desperately to disappear, because after staring at Ollie, all eyes inevitably turned to the girl he was strutting around.

"Yeah, that's definitely not it," I said once he was finished with his little performance.

He pouted in response.

"So what then?" he asked, slightly out of breath as he followed me over to one of the only shaded spots left in the school yard. It was lunchtime and we'd scarfed down our food so that we could find a quiet place to work out the next phase of our plan. Doing this at school wasn't exactly ideal. But we were sort of in a time crunch, and Ollie seemed incapable of talking about anything else when I was around, so certain concessions needed to be made. This was one of them.

"It's really not a big deal," I explained. "He just sort of freaked when I told him my only friend here was a *guy*. He's pulling the protective parent card and thinks something's going on."

"Ew," Ollie said, making a face.

"That's what I said." I mirrored his reaction. "So I thought if he just *met* you, then he'd realize he has nothing to worry about and things can go back to normal. Well, as normal as can be expected in my life."

Ollie seemed lost in thought, and for a few seconds he just stared off into space.

"What *does* one wear to meet a detective?" he asked finally, musing out loud. Then, he added, "Don't worry, I'll figure something out."

"Oh, thank gosh," I said. "Because *that's* what I was worried about. Not the whole getting-ready-to-steal-from-one-of-the-wealthiest-people-in-Greenwich stuff. Or you possibly letting all that slip in an attempt to make friendly conversation. Yes, I was afraid I'd be kept up at night stressed over whether you'll choose purple or yellow pants when you meet my uncle for the first time."

"Your sarcasm is noted and not appreciated," Ollie said pointedly. "And I'd never wear yellow. It completely washes me out."

"*Of course* it does," I said with a sigh. "Can we please talk about the gala now?"

"I thought we already were," Ollie said. "I told you, I refuse to wear yellow."

"Not that part," I said, wanting desperately to change topics. "There are a lot of things we still need to work out before we show up at Miles's house."

Ollie began to reach into his bag and pull out a piece of paper and a pen, but I waved him off.

"A thief never leaves evidence of her plan," I reminded him. "No paper trails in public. This is where you have to start developing a good memory. Because there's a lot you're going to have to remember once we get going."

"What about that *Mission: Impossible* stuff? Like, can I write it down and just make it self-destruct later?" Ollie asked, still holding the pad of paper in his hand.

"Do you know how to make a piece of paper self-destruct?" I asked him.

"No," he said blankly.

"Then I guess we can't do the *Mission: Impossible* stuff, can we?" I answered. "You'll just have to start using that noggin for something other than storing useless pop trivia."

"Hey, that useless trivia led me to you," he said defensively.

"My point exactly," I said. "Let's start filling that head with more *practical* info. Like how to pickpocket."

Ollie's eyes grew wide with excitement.

"Yeeeesss." He let the word out slowly. "*That's* what I'm talking about. When do I learn that?"

"Oh, *you* won't actually be the one stealing anything," I corrected him. "I'll be doing that. But you can be my distraction."

"I still get to do something, right?" he asked hopefully.

"Yes, your part is especially important to the whole plan," I said seriously. And this was technically true. Having a distraction would make stealing from Miles that much easier.

"Okay," Ollie said, seeming satisfied. "What else?"

"I'm reaching out to my hacker guy to have him dig into Miles's financials a bit before we go in, to narrow down our targets," I said.

"You have a hacker guy?" Ollie asked.

"I have a guy for everything," I said. Then I added, "Don't you?"

Ollie thought about this. "I have a stylist."

"Great. I'll let you know when I need a new look," I said. "In the meantime, I'll also get my guy to start working on a replica of Miles's current phone and case, so we can take his to see if there's anything incriminating on it. Oh, and we need something to help out with the voice and fingerprint recognition for the treasure room."

I hesitated before bringing up the next part of our plan. Not because it was profoundly difficult or anything, but because I knew after I did, I wouldn't get another word in edgewise.

"Lastly, we need to get costumes together," I said quickly, hoping he'd at least let me finish before losing his cool. "We can go tomorrow after school to look for something. We shouldn't rent anything, because it could be traced back to us—"

Ollie's eyes had grown wide as I talked and he was fidgeting around like he needed to go to the bathroom.

"Let me do it!" The words burst out of him like a balloon that had been given one too many puffs of air.

I looked around to see if anyone else had heard Ollie's outburst, but for once, nobody was paying attention to us. Still, I knew if I didn't answer him, there would be more exclamations and it likely wouldn't remain that way. So I opened my mouth to respond, only to be cut off before I could get anything out.

"Frankie, *please* let me do this," Ollie begged. Then his face grew serious. "Look, you know all this thieving stuff, I'll be the first to admit that. In that arena, *you're* the boss. You make the rules. And I'm happy to be your faithful sidekick on that. But this? Fashion? Costumes? Dressing up? That is my *life*. Nobody can do a better job than me of creating a look."

I cocked my head to the side. "But the point is not to stand out, Ollie," I argued. "And I know you. You don't do subtle."

Ollie grinned at that. "But that's the great thing about this. It's a *masquerade gala*. The point is to go big, otherwise we *will* stand out. Get it? This is a fundraiser for rich people. And that means they're going to have their costumes created by big-time designers and stuff like that. We can't go in looking like we made our outfits in home ec, or they'll know we don't belong. We have to come legit."

When he put it that way, I realized he was right. We'd have to step up our game in order to fly under the radar at the masquerade. And as much as I hated handing over any part of the plan to someone who had no previous experience with pulling off a con, I knew Ollie could get the job done.

Plus, I *had* to give him something to do. He wasn't going to be involved that much in the rest of the operation, and this would keep him from bothering me about that. Which would leave me open to focusing on the rest of what had to be done.

The important parts.

"*Fine*," I said, making it sound like I was conceding

on something I didn't want to. "But nothing too crazy. Keep it within the confines of the event, okay?"

"Deal," he said, looking like a kid on Christmas day. Then he stood up and started prancing around as he talked out loud to himself about all the different options worthy of a high-class gala.

I took this as my chance to focus on my own stuff and pulled out my burner phone to compose an email. But before I could even navigate through the passcode to unlock it, I felt a spray of liquid hit me across the face and arms.

I inhaled sharply and jumped up, thinking that maybe a sprinkler had gone off nearby accidentally, but when I looked up, I saw that Ollie was standing there stock-still, arms outstretched, and with his back to me.

"What was that?" I asked him, trying not to shriek.

Then my eyes focused just beyond my friend and landed on a pack of girls standing about five feet away. There were four of them all together, and each held what appeared to be a now-empty paper cup. A variety of different-colored liquids stained the ground below. I looked at the brown, pink, and white spots decorating the area leading up to them, and as my gaze drifted upward, I noticed that Annabelle was holding the biggest cup.

"What the—" I started to say, but lost the words as Ollie turned around in slow motion.

That's when I realized I'd barely gotten splashed. Ollie, however, had received the full brunt of their assault. With milk shake dripping from his eyelashes, he looked at me with such surprise on his face that I wondered whether he'd gone into shock. Which wouldn't have been too big a stretch, considering he was covered from head to toe with the frosty treats.

"We don't believe in wearing fur," Annabelle said when my eyes finally met hers. "My family's a supporter of PETA, you know. And those poor, defenseless animals didn't deserve to be made into . . . *that*."

She made a face as she pointed at Ollie's jacket like it was a decaying bear carcass.

"Are you blind, Annabelle?" Ollie asked, still holding his arms away from his body. "This isn't *fur*. It's freaking *wool*!"

Annabelle squinted as if she could somehow see around the globs of milk shake to the material underneath. After a second, she just shrugged. "Wool still comes from an animal. Besides, I did you a favor. It was totes uggo anyway."

I opened my mouth to say something but then paused. It wasn't because I was afraid. Not of confronting Annabelle, and certainly not of what she might do to me if I did. It was more the fact that the thief in me was screaming not to reveal myself. If I stood up to Annabelle now, any cards I'd been holding that made the rest of the students see me as—well, nonthreatening—would be shown. They'd suddenly *know* I was smarter than them. Stronger than them. So much more than them. And that I'd been successfully hiding who I was the whole time.

And that would lead to them wondering what else I was hiding.

Which was the last thing I wanted.

Before I had a chance to make a decision on what to do next, Annabelle took a step toward Ollie and touched a sticky spot on his arm with one finger.

"Maybe you should think more carefully when choosing who you hang out with, Ollie," she said, looking straight at me as she said it. "If you hang out with trash, you might be mistaken for trash. And we take out our trash *here*."

My mouth dropped open as she tossed her cup at Ollie's feet and promptly started to walk off. Each of the other girls followed her lead and deposited her empty drink on the ground near Ollie too.

By the time they'd disappeared, I was shaking with anger and cursing under my breath.

Ollie remained frozen in place for a minute but then slowly began to peel off his formerly beautiful jacket, which was now soaked in dairy. The white outfit he wore underneath was spattered with different shades of color, and not in a creative, this-was-the-look-I-was-going-for way.

His outfit, like his mood, had been destroyed.

And because I'd been more concerned about how it would all affect me, I hadn't done a thing to stop it.

Entry Thirty

"The best pickpockets in the world are all about controlling people's attention," I explained to Ollie as he sat cross-legged on my bed, eyes glued to me.

I was pacing around my room like a teacher at the front of the class. I'd even brought out a whiteboard, where I'd written *Pickpocketing 101* in big black letters, underlined twice.

Not that Ollie needed the reminder. He knew why we were here. He'd been talking about it all day long, totally psyched that he was about to learn one of his first practical thieving skills.

And I knew how he felt. The nervousness and jitters that bubble up when you're about to do something wrong. Then the excitement of actually being able to pull it off. I still get that slightly queasy feeling in my stomach every time I do it, even though I have seven years of experience under my belt.

Ollie was learning the skills pretty late for a thief. I myself had been given my first lesson at the age of five. Dad had worked with me on a single grab-and-go for over a month. He'd refused to even let me try it out on anyone outside our circle until I'd successfully stolen his wallet ten times in a row.

But man, from my very first time doing it out in the real world, I was hooked.

After that, I'd practiced as often as I could. And I'd gotten good. Like, *super* good. I'd even managed to impress my dad, which was hard to do, considering he wasn't exactly a slouch in that department himself.

But as much as I was an expert on the art of pick-pocketing, I'd never actually *taught* anyone else to do it.

And truth be told, I wasn't sure I'd be any good at it.

Luckily, Ollie just needed to know the fundamentals. I'd be doing the real work, after all. But it was still good for him to know how it all worked. If he knew what was going on, he'd be less likely to screw it up for us in front of Miles.

"If you can control a person's attention, you can control the person. In fact, a great pickpocket is a lot like a really good magician. They're all about sleight of hand," I said, holding my palms up in front of me to show Ollie that they were empty.

"Misdirection," I said.

With a quick flick of my wrist, I closed my fist, suddenly producing a paper clip as if out of thin air and holding it up for him to see. His eyes grew wide.

"And then making things disappear," I finished, and blew on the paper clip, making it vanish as I held my hands up for him again.

Ollie's grin widened and he began clapping for me with glee. I almost felt bad at how easy it was to trick him. But I had to admit, it *did* sort of feel satisfying to finally be able to show someone—outside of my family—what I was capable of.

I turned my back to Ollie and walked over to the whiteboard.

"Now, what I'm going to teach you today can work for stealing most things off a person," I said. "A cell phone, a wallet, a watch—each of these items can be snatched using different variations of the same trick."

Ollie nodded enthusiastically and leaned forward as if this would somehow help him figure out what I was going to do next.

"We'll be working together on the grab-and-replace of Miles's cell phone on gala night. I think it's important for you to see firsthand how easy it can be to be stolen from. Even when the situation is one-on-one and you know what the person's about to do. Stand up and I'll show you."

Ollie almost fell over in his haste to get off the bed but steadied himself as he made his way over to me. I could tell he was excited. Heck, *I* was excited. It had been a while since I'd worked on any of the tricks of my trade. At least six months now. Ever since Dad had been arrested and my life had been turned upside down.

But I knew it would be like riding a bike. You never forget how to do it.

"Okay, so we're going to start with the basics," I said, handing Ollie a watch, a wallet, and one of the burner phones. I walked absently in a semicircle as he slipped the timepiece around his wrist and then tucked the cell into his back pocket and the wallet into the left front pocket of his fitted jeans. "Make sure it's all secure. All right, you ready?"

Ollie nodded and took a stance like we were about to play a game of tag—legs slightly apart, bent just at the knee, and arms up in front of his body offensively.

"What are you doing?" I asked.

"Nothing," he said, his face blank.

"You're standing weird," I said, placing a hand on my hip.

"No, I'm not," Ollie said, still posing awkwardly in front of me. "This is how I always stand."

I rolled my eyes.

"You do not," I said, annoyed. With a sigh, I stepped toward him and grabbed hold of his arms, forcing him to stand up straighter. Then, switching my grip over to just one wrist, I kicked apart his legs until he was standing like a regular person. "There. Now you don't look like a linebacker ready to take me down. Wait, why is your collar doing that funky, tweaky thing . . ."

I reached across him to touch his shoulder and began to pick at the material there.

"What tweaky thing?" Ollie asked, and turned to see what I was talking about, just as I was finishing getting him straightened up. When I was done, I brushed off his shoulder and took a step back to look at him.

194

"There we go," I said, nodding. "That's better."

"Okay," Ollie said with a smile. "Now that *that's* over. Show me what you've got, Lorde. No way you're pulling one over on me."

"Where's your watch, Ollie?" I asked him.

"It's on my—" Ollie began to say as he lifted his wrist to show me the timepiece he'd attached to himself earlier.

But there was nothing there.

When he looked back at me, I pulled his watch out of my pocket triumphantly and held it up for him to see.

"No. Freaking. *Way,*" Ollie breathed, like I'd just made the house around us disappear. "How did you do that?"

I tossed the watch back to him.

"Like I said before. If you control a person's attention, you control the person."

"Do it again," he begged as he replaced the watch. "I bet you can't do it again."

"Ollie, we could be here all day, me just stealing from you," I said, the thought sounding slightly fun but also tedious. "How about I just *show* you how I did it and we move on."

Ollie nodded eagerly and I began to share my secrets with him.

"First off, the weird way you were standing was actually helpful. It gave me a reason to come into your personal space and make contact with you," I said, stepping toward him and grabbing hold of his arms like I had before. "Now I have an *excuse* to touch you."

I pulled him up straighter to show him what I meant.

"Then, while still remaining in physical contact, I slide this hand down to cover your wrist and watch while stepping back to look down at your feet. Keeping that constant connection with you is key, because it allows me to start working the latch on the watch without you realizing I'm doing it," I said, wiggling my fingers around the clasp expertly. "And the reason you don't realize I'm doing it, is because now I've changed the focus from what I'm doing up here to what I'm doing down there. That's part one of the misdirection."

Ollie couldn't help but look down as I slid my foot in between his and kicked his legs apart slightly.

"See, your brain's only able to focus on one thing at a time, so when I force you to focus on what I'm doing to your legs, your brain is completely ignoring the fact that I'm working one of my fingers under the watchband."

As I revealed this, Ollie looked back up at his wrist and seemed shocked to see my finger stuck between the strap and his skin.

"Hey!" he said, surprised.

"And now we move on to misdirection number two," I explained, leaning in and grabbing his collar with my free hand. His head instinctively followed my arm, even though he was already aware of what was coming next. As I continued to fiddle with his shirt, I finished unlatching the watch from his wrist but held it in place for the moment. "And finally I retrieve the item without you noticing anything's amiss."

I stepped back and held up my hands up in a sort of "ta-dah" moment. They were empty. But then again, so was Ollie's arm.

He looked at me questioningly until I pulled the nicked watch out of my back pocket.

"Let me try! Let me try!" he said, jumping up and down.

I tried not to laugh but couldn't help myself.

"Okay," I said, giving in more easily than I'd planned to. The truth was, I could remember the excitement I'd felt when I was first starting out, and I sympathized. "But only a few times. We're not even stealing Miles's watch, so practicing this is a waste of time. A grab-and-replace is much more involved than a grab-and-go. And we have to make sure everything goes off seamlessly."

"Ooooh, I want to see *that* one," Ollie said, dropping the watch onto the floor, along with his interest in what I'd just shown him. "The grab-and-replace. Do it on me. Do it on me!"

"Down, boy," I said, trying my best to calm him. Then, with a sly smile, I took another step toward him and prepared to show him my next trick. "Okay, *this* is how we're going to steal from Christian Miles. . . ."

Entry Thirty-One

"So what's this kid's last name again?" Uncle Scotty asked as he moved around the kitchen, pulling plates and utensils out and placing them on the counter.

It was Friday night and Ollie was coming over for dinner. It felt uncomfortably like when you brought a date to meet your parents for the first time. Only, there was nothing between Ollie and me except for what one *might* call a budding friendship.

It was still going to be awkward, though. I could just tell.

"Um, Santiago, I think?" I said, peeking inside the two large pizza boxes that had been placed in the middle of the table.

"You don't know your friend's last name?" Uncle Scotty asked, giving me an incredulous look.

"It's middle school," I said by way of explanation. "Apparently, we don't exactly do formal introductions? I'm finding that kids my age operate more on a need-to-know basis."

Which, if I'm being honest, is more my speed anyway. The less the other kids know about me, the better.

"Right," Uncle Scotty said, though he didn't seem to buy it. "So what *do* you know about this kid?"

"The *kid's* name is Ollie," I reminded him as I hopped

up onto the counter to sit. "And I don't know. He's like, really *theatrical*. An actor. Or he wants to be, anyway. I'm not actually sure he's been in anything before."

"An actor?" Uncle Scotty asked, snorting. "Please don't tell me he's the James Dean type?"

"Who's James Dean?" I asked blankly.

Uncle Scotty looked up at the ceiling and muttered something under his breath while shaking his head.

"I forget how young you are sometimes," he said, barely loud enough for me to hear. But then he cleared his throat and spoke up. "James Dean was this actor from the fifties who was known for his brooding bad-boy behavior and too-cool-for-school attitude—"

"Ollie is *not* like that James guy," I said, cutting him off there. "More like James Corden."

Uncle Scotty raised an eyebrow at that but didn't ask me to explain.

"So where does this actor, Ollie, live?" he asked, moving on.

"Don't know," I answered, kicking my legs as I sat on the counter. "Never been to his house."

"What's his family like?"

"Not sure," I said. "I've never asked."

"What's his favorite color?" Uncle Scotty asked, sounding exasperated.

"Ooh, ooh! I know what color he *doesn't* like," I said, like this was something to be proud of. "Yellow. Apparently it totally washes him out."

Uncle Scotty stopped what he was doing to stare at me. "Seriously?" he asked.

I nodded.

He walked from the counter and over to me. "Are you sure this guy's even your friend?" he asked. "It seems like you don't really know anything about him."

The comment came as a surprise. Not because Uncle Scotty was *wrong*, but because he was sort of right. I knew plenty of surface stuff about Ollie. He wanted to be an actor. He liked fashion. That sort of thing. But when it got down to the important stuff—the stuff that I was pretty sure friends were supposed to know about each other—I didn't actually know that much.

And now that Uncle Scotty had brought it up, his questions were forcing me to really look at why I was willing to let Ollie into the thieving side of my life but not into the rest of it. Logically, I knew it was partly because I'd always been taught that if you really let a person into your life, you left yourself vulnerable and open to being a target.

And I wasn't about to be a target.

This rule of never getting close to anyone has never applied to my dad, of course. I've never had to worry about him knowing the real me, and he's never kept me from knowing the real him. But that's a different situation completely.

Friends, on the other hand. That's a more complicated subject.

Dad had told me enough horror stories about being double-crossed by friends in his early thieving days for me to be wary of trusting anyone outside the family circle. But the truth was, I'd just never really had the chance to make friends before. Between our questionable lifestyle, the constant reinventions of ourselves with every con, and the fact that we were always moving on to the next city or country, it was pretty tough to find anyone my age that I wanted to spend time getting to know, let alone anyone I was willing to let get to know me.

But now here was Ollie.

It was different with him for so many reasons. First, he'd known who I was before I'd even shown up at school. This alone was something I wasn't used to. Everywhere I'd gone in the past, I'd been relatively anonymous. Nobody knew who I was, therefore I could be anybody I chose to be. But here in Greenwich, Ollie had known my biggest secret from the start—my real identity.

And now somehow he'd become my partner in crime.

Yet I was still so hesitant to get close to him. Heck, I didn't even know his favorite color.

And until now, I'd been perfectly content with our friendship being one-sided. But I was beginning to see that I was about to trust my life to a relative stranger, and somehow that no longer sat well with me.

The truth was, I didn't know my partner.

I didn't know my friend.

And that fact made me feel . . . *sad.*

At that precise moment, there was a knock at the front door. It was that knock where you expect the person on the other side to finish with two sharp raps.

I hopped down from the counter and skipped quickly over to the front door to swing it open.

"Ollie!" I screamed, overcompensating for how guilty I was suddenly feeling. "Come on in!"

I waved him inside and gave him a big smile. Only, I rarely smiled for no reason and I was fairly sure the smile I was giving off right then was bordering on creepy.

Ollie gave me a look that said I was right. My face fell back into its usual disaffected look.

"We got pizza," I said, less enthusiastically.

"Sweet!" Ollie said, and swept past me and into the kitchen. I watched as he walked right up to my uncle and held out his hand. "It's a pleasure to meet you, Detective Lorde."

Uncle Scotty glanced over at me as if to say *What's going on?* but shook Ollie's hand anyway. I just shrugged and gestured back like the grandness of Ollie's greeting was completely normal.

And it was. For Ollie. I thought back to the first time I'd met him, and almost laughed.

At least he hadn't bowed to my uncle like he had to me.

Five minutes later, the three of us were seated at the kitchen table and shoving gooey slices of pizza into our mouths. In true Ollie fashion, he hadn't stopped talking since he'd arrived, and every once in a while Uncle Scotty would look over at me like he was expecting me to bail him out.

I ignored him, because, well, he was the one who wanted to get to know my new friend. And he was getting what he'd asked for.

Well, kind of.

"So have you ever shot anyone?" Ollie asked Uncle Scotty, his eyes wide with curiosity. It was about the twentieth question Ollie had asked since we'd sat down to eat, and I could tell that my uncle was growing tired of the nonstop interrogation.

"Um, I can't really talk about the investigations I've worked on," Uncle Scotty said, trying to evade the question. I knew this wasn't totally true. Yes, Uncle Scotty couldn't talk about an *ongoing* investigation. But all the other stuff was fair game. He just didn't *want* to talk about it.

I let out a little laugh at the whole situation and Uncle Scotty used it as an excuse to change the subject.

"How about you, Ollie?" he said, trying to take control. "You have a lot of questions about what it's like to be a cop. Any interest in pursuing law enforcement once you graduate?"

Ollie and I looked at each other and burst out laughing.

"What's so funny?" Uncle Scotty asked.

"You do *not* want to give Ollie a badge," I said, still laughing.

Ollie was shaking his head at the thought. "It's true. My middle name *so* isn't Danger," he said.

"What *is* your middle name?" I asked, remembering that I wanted to be more proactive in learning these little details about Ollie.

Ollie paused for a moment, like my question had taken him by surprise.

"Domingo," he answered finally. Then he turned back to Uncle Scotty. "My interest is more in the sense of, I wouldn't mind *playing* a cop on TV one day," he explained. "Although, on second thought, those blue uniforms really bum me out."

"Maybe you could star as some sort of offbeat detective or something," I suggested. "Like that show about the psychic detective. Or you could play a detective to the stars."

"Those don't actually exist," Uncle Scotty cut in.

"I *like* it," Ollie said dreamily. Then he waved his hands through the air while looking off into space like he could picture it. "Ollie Santiago is *The Star Detective*. Coming Tuesday nights on NBC."

"Okay, guys," Uncle Scotty said, clearly sorry he'd brought it up in the first place.

"*The Star Detective:* Where fashion is a *crime*," I added dramatically.

"Oh, geez," Uncle Scotty said, placing his head in his hands like he was giving up. After a moment, he picked up his cell phone and studied it, even though I was pretty sure it hadn't made a sound. "Oh, would you look at that. Looks like the station needs me for . . . something. You guys good to finish up here?"

He stood up, not waiting for us to answer, and took his plate over to the sink.

When he turned back to us, it was clear he was ready to bolt.

"Don't worry, Uncle Scotty," I said, raising my eyebrow a bit just to show him I knew what he was really up to. "We can clean up here. You go take care of that . . . *important case* you've been working on."

"Thanks, kiddo," Uncle Scotty said with obvious relief. "Nice to meet you, Ollie. You're welcome over here anytime."

"Thank you, sir," Ollie said, scrambling to wipe his greasy hands on his napkin so he could shake my uncle's hand again. "Maybe we can talk more about your job next time. I have so many other questions."

Uncle Scotty gestured for Ollie to remain seated and just gave him a friendly little wave before heading over to the front door.

"Sounds good," he said quickly before disappearing into the night and leaving the two of us alone.

After a minute, Ollie grabbed another slice of pizza and wrinkled up his nose. "You know, for a detective, your uncle doesn't ask a lot of questions," he mused out loud. "I mean, I just had to keep talking, and talking, and *talking* . . ."

I shook my head and began to laugh.

Entry Thirty-Two

In the history of my entire time as a thief, never have I *ever* worn feathers on a job.

I know. Surprising, right?

That was sarcasm. It shouldn't be surprising at all. Who, in real life, ever finds the appropriate occasion to wear dead bird fur?

Well, the answer to that would be: Ollie.

Ollie Santiago would probably argue that any occasion calls for a feather or two.

"You're crushing them!" he whined for about the tenth time since we'd stuffed ourselves into the cab.

"There's no other way for me to sit in this outfit," I argued, but shifted my weight over to my right hip in an attempt to give the back of my dress more real estate on the backseat. "Maybe you should've thought of that when you designed this . . . thing."

"It's not a *thing*," Ollie said, shooting me a look over his shoulder. In an attempt not to ruin his own outfit, he was kneeling on the back seat, facing out the rear window. It had been the only way the two of us had been able to fit into the car at the same time. "It's a work of art."

"Well, your *art* is annoying," I said.

"It wasn't meant to sit down in," he informed me, like

this fact should've been obvious. "It was meant to wow, while still serving a purpose. Believe me, you'll thank me later when you find that you have plenty of room up under there for . . . *stuff.*"

Ollie glanced back toward the driver to see if he was listening to our conversation. The guy had the radio tuned to some kind of international station and was bobbing his head along to what sounded like a Latin pop song. But I knew that just because someone looks preoccupied doesn't mean they aren't listening to every word you say.

Still, I wasn't worried. Between our masks, the fake accents we were already practicing, and the fact that I'd be paying the driver in cash, none of it would matter if we stood out to him.

Because we were just about up to Miles's circular driveway and the cabbie was about to see that we weren't the only weirdos dressed up incognito.

"Holy Met Gala," Ollie breathed as we slowed to allow a bunch of guests to cross in front of the cab on their way to the entrance of Miles Manor.

And he wasn't wrong. What we saw around us was like walking into a fairy tale.

Or Comic-Con.

Either way, every single person there had brought their A game.

I'd been nervous when Ollie had revealed our costumes earlier that night. I'd thought they were too extravagant, too over-the-top. I'd argued that we would stand out so much that all eyes would be glued to us, making it impossible to do what we were there to do.

But now I had to admit that Ollie had been right. He'd been one hundred percent right, actually. Because every costume I was seeing was like a masterpiece meant to showcase each designer's fantastical whims. Every possible shade of the rainbow danced around us, creating an effect like a disco ball and making my eyes swim. The fabrics were just as mesmerizing, ranging from taffeta and velvet to animal skin and jewels.

In this sea of unlimited imagination, no single pearl was going to stand out. Each was perfect in its own right.

"I take it all back," I said as I watched a woman take calculated steps up Miles's stairs, careful not to trip over her own outfit. She looked like a living, breathing Picasso painting. Her dress was sort of deconstructed, half of it missing but replaced with pieces of material in the shape of body parts. An eyeball here. Pink, pouty lips there. They all appeared to cling to her body as if they'd been glued on. As if the rest of her outfit wasn't odd enough, she was wearing a tower of different-sized top hats, balancing precariously on her head. It was completely compelling and completely bizarre at the same time.

"I will never doubt you when it comes to party attire again," I said to Ollie, fully meaning it.

"That's all I ask," he responded, a grin appearing on his face. "Now, let's get this gala started, shall we?"

The cab had finally stopped and a man in a tuxedo was waving for us to get out of the car and join the throngs of other guests making their way into the party. When we didn't immediately comply, he jogged over to us and held the door open with one hand while reaching in to offer me his other.

I took it gratefully. I wasn't sure how I would get out otherwise. Ollie had put me in platform pumps that were at least six inches tall. It was going to take all my energy just to keep from falling over in them. But as Ollie explained, it would hide my true height, which would make it that much more difficult to identify me later.

As I slipped out of the car, I left every part of the old me behind. I was no longer Frankie Lorde, part-time international thief, part-time middle school student. I had transformed into Raven, the sleek, dark beauty who belonged at this fundraising gala. Raven oozed money and power. Her nationality was hard to place on account of the mixed accent I'd come up with over the course of the past week: a blend of Russian and Australian. I knew that no matter how much anyone tried to place it, they wouldn't be able to.

And this added to the mystery that was Raven.

Nothing ruffled her feathers, and she could take off at any moment, disappearing into the night.

The outfit had been a perfect choice on Ollie's part. And ingeniously assembled, I had to admit. Though nobody but me would ever know it, the crinoline under the skirt of the dress—the structure meant to make it pouf out in the back like a bird's tail feathers—was constructed a lot like a birdcage. Dozens of springy steel rods encircled the lower half of my body, starting at my waist and spreading out three feet behind me.

Directly on top of that lay the actual material of the dress, topped by thousands of delicate, sleek black feathers. Ollie swore they weren't real, but they sure looked like it. The top was form-fitting, with a sweetheart neckline, and the arms billowed out like wings that only appeared when I lifted my arms.

Covering the majority of my face was an even more beautiful mask, made of the same feathers and adorned with a few well-placed black jewels. There was no way to tell it was me underneath, but even so, I'd put in graphite-colored contacts, making it appear as if my eyes were the color of night.

In the end, I looked . . . wild and otherworldly.

It was absolutely incredible without being too flashy.

Ollie's outfit, on the other hand? Well, that was a different story entirely.

Because he had come as none other than a peacock.

The blend of bright blues, greens, teals, and the occasional flash of gold weaved themselves around Ollie's body expertly, one color fading into the next like an optical illusion.

His pants were made from the darkest part of the bird's feathers, giving the appearance that all the color in the room was cascading from the top of him downward until it disappeared into the ground below. His jacket jutted out at the waist, similar to a peplum top, and it made him look even more like the peacock he was emulating. A row of feathers created a tiny halo just behind his shoulders, giving another shot of color to the overall look.

But that wasn't the showstopper. The thing that would make Ollie's outfit extraordinary would come later.

And I for one couldn't wait to see it.

Especially since it was an important key to pulling this whole thing off.

As I stepped away from the car, the sea of people seemed to part, allowing me to make my way toward the entrance. After a few steps, I felt Ollie's presence by my side. And then, as if we'd choreographed it, I held out my hand and he took it like we were a flock that only flew together.

Eyes turned toward us. There might've been some whispering, possibly even some pointing. I refused to smile, even though inside I was satisfied with the reaction.

But just as quickly as we'd come to be the center of attention, the other partygoers were already beginning to move on to the next elaborate outfit. And the next.

With a final glance behind us, we entered the party without much more fanfare or anyone remembering we'd come at all.

Entry Thirty-Three

Miles's house looked pretty much the way it had the last time Ollie and I had been there. Cavernous, expensive, clean—the way you would expect a house of that stature to look. As soon as we handed over our invitation to the security team, we were ushered through the archway under the stairs and onward until we were again outside.

In Miles's backyard, we walked underneath a canopy of stars and twinkle lights that had been hung by the hundreds around his expansive property. The back deck area had been set up like an elaborate dance hall, and a live orchestra played music softly from somewhere I couldn't pinpoint. Waiters walked around supplying people with drinks and tiny bites of food that weren't immediately recognizable.

"Caviar and crème fraîche tartlet?" A man in a black-and-white waiter's uniform appeared in front of us, proffering a tray of round black-and-white things.

"Cheers," Ollie said, taking one of the tartlets eagerly.

"I'm not sure you want—" I started to say to him as he put the thing up to his lips and almost swallowed it whole.

A few chews later and Ollie had frozen in place before

putting his napkin to his mouth and trying to discreetly spit out the remnants.

"Told you," I said, a tiny smile appearing on my lips.

"What *was* that?" he asked, disgusted.

"Basically, sour cream and fish eggs," I answered.

"What the—" Ollie sputtered, taking a glass of water off a passing tray and gulping it down. "Why would they *serve* that?"

"Because each one of those cost about two hundred dollars a pop," I said, keeping my voice down as we moved through the party.

"That's insane," he whispered.

"That's the life of the rich and famous," I replied.

"Country foie gras toasts with pickled grapes?" a different waiter offered, displaying his tray in front of Ollie and me.

"Do I want this?" Ollie asked me.

I slowly shook my head.

"No thanks," Ollie said to the guy sullenly. When the waiter was gone, he asked, "What was it?"

"Fatty duck liver," I said.

"Aren't rich people supposed to eat *better* than the rest of us?" he asked, shaking his head.

"You'd think," I said, continuing to mingle, all the while searching for Miles.

When we finally found him, he was already deep into the crowd. Nearly backed into a corner near the balcony that overlooked the pool and beyond, the blond-haired billionaire was animatedly talking to someone who was dressed up like a life-sized Oscar statue.

Discreetly positioning Ollie in front of me as a cover, I studied Miles as he interacted with people. Every few minutes or so someone new would approach him, cutting into whatever conversation he'd had going on. Like a well-oiled machine, he would politely excuse himself from whoever he was talking to in order to schmooze with the new potential donor for roughly two minutes before moving on to the next. There was no visible line of people waiting to talk to him, but after ten minutes or so, I knew that there would be no shortage of guests looking to take up his time.

That meant I was going to have to cut in if I wanted my two minutes with the real estate mogul.

And I needed every bit of those two minutes to do what I had to do.

A man had just wandered up to Miles and shook his hand before introducing him to his lady friend, who was lit up like a Christmas tree—literally.

"I'm going in," I said to Ollie, never taking my eyes off Miles.

"Already?" he asked, his voice coming out in a squeak.

"You don't have to do this," I reminded him. I felt like I needed to give Ollie one last out. A chance to keep his side of the road clean. An opportunity *not* to turn out like me.

And for a second, I thought he might take it. Part of me hoped he would take it.

But he didn't.

Instead, he stood up as straight as his outfit would allow and jutted his chin out with resolve.

"No, I'm ready," he said, sounding more confident than I knew he felt.

"Really, Ollie," I said quietly, catching his eye. "I can do the rest of it on my own."

Ollie shook his head and forced a smile. "And let you have all the fun? Yeah, right."

I smiled and took hold of his hand as I brushed past him. Then, with a reassuring squeeze, I left him standing there as I walked toward Miles.

"Mr. Miles," I said, coming up behind him. The words came out low and confident. With the accent and a new raspiness I'd added to my voice, there was no way I'd be mistaken for a schoolgirl.

"Yes?" he responded before he'd even turned around to see who was talking to him.

As his eyes fell on me, though, I saw them widen in surprise before settling into his trademark laid-back, overly confident look. It was brief, but I'd been watching his face for any reaction and was happy my entrance had had its intended effect.

"I'm sorry, Gary," he said to the man he'd been talking to, though his gaze never left my face. "It was really great to meet you, but duty calls."

The man looked disappointed but nodded like he understood.

"Oh, of—of course. Y-yeah," he stammered, glancing sideways at his date and looking embarrassed to be dismissed in front of her. "I'll just, uh . . . find you later."

"Sounds good," Miles said, though I could tell he'd already forgotten about the guy.

And then we were alone.

Well, as alone as we could be with several of Miles's bodyguards standing mere feet away and a few hundred guests milling around us.

"I'm Christian Miles," he said, though it was clear he expected me to already know who he was. "And you are?"

He held out his hand, but I didn't take it. I was in control of this situation.

"Let's just say I'm a fan of your work," I said, letting a tiny smile escape my lips.

"Really?" Miles said, his eyes twinkling with delight. "And what have I done to earn your admiration?"

I shoved my hands into the hidden pockets of my dress and shrugged coyly.

That was Ollie's cue to get moving—me placing my hands in my pockets—and I knew he would be approaching us soon. And that meant things were about to happen real fast.

Inside my pockets, I wrapped my fingers around the duplicate cell phone while pressing Record on the device I was holding in my other hand.

"Oh, *you* know," I said. "All the charity work you're a part of."

216

"Ahhh, yes, that," he said, waving it off like it wasn't a big deal.

"I think it's so . . . *heroic* when people of your stature use their fortunes to help others," I said, reaching out and picking a piece of lint off his jacket. "You should really consider starting your own foundation, you know? The Christian Miles Foundation, maybe? I could be your first supporter."

Miles's eyes followed my hand as I pulled away.

"I like that. *The Christian Miles Foundation,*" he mused out loud. "But I've learned over the years to leave certain things up to the experts. Besides, there are plenty of *other* things I'm good at."

Barf.

Like swindling hardworking people out of their money, I wanted to say, but stayed focused.

"So I've heard," I said, nodding.

"Mr. Miles! Mr. Miles!" I heard Ollie call out in his fake British accent. My back was to him, but I could imagine him waddling up to Miles, every bit the opposite of my polished elegance.

As Miles's attention was pulled toward Ollie, I turned as well, trying my best to give off an air of disgust and annoyance at the person interrupting us. Miles saw my reaction and winked at me. Ew.

"I'm really sorry about this," he muttered to me. "Everyone wants their five minutes, you know . . . I'll get rid of him."

"No," I said, sounding reluctant. "If it helps the charity . . ."

"Mr. Miles!" Ollie said, sounding slightly out of breath from the whole production. "I just wanted to say what an honor it is to have been invited to such a smashing event. Really *smashing*."

I forced my face to remain neutral, though I was tempted to laugh at how thick Ollie was laying it on.

And to his credit, he was actually doing a great job. I could see Miles's face begin to redden with embarrassment.

"Well, thank you," Miles said, clearing his throat and shooting a hurried glance over at his security team, who were standing by silently. "We're very happy you could attend. But if you could please excuse me—"

At this, one of the beefy-looking guards started to move toward Ollie, and I fought the urge to shoot my friend a warning look. If they shuffled him out of there too quickly, I'd have to change the plan, and that would bring all sorts of unexpected variables to the situation.

As if reading my mind, Ollie quickly moved into the space that Miles and I had been sharing, nearly pushing me out of the way in the process.

"And the idea of a masquerade ball? Well, I just had a jolly good time coming up with my costume." Ollie continued to jabber on as if I didn't exist. "In fact, well, you've just got to see this!"

Before any of us could stop him, Ollie reached up to his neckline and pulled on a cord that had been hiding

218

inside his jacket. Suddenly, a four-foot halo of feathers fanned out around his backside, looking exactly like a peacock's tail. It was magnificent, and I knew it was a showstopping moment for Ollie. He'd been so proud when he'd told me about it, and part of me wanted nothing more than to halt everything and enjoy it with him. But then, as I'd been expecting, one side of his tail fell on top of me, knocking me forward and into Miles's arms.

I grabbed on to Miles's jacket clumsily as I fought to keep from completely face-planting on the ground.

"Oh, my!" Ollie exclaimed, watching as we stumbled over each other. Then, as if he were looking for help, he turned his whole body away, covering the two of us in tail feathers again and preventing anyone from seeing what we were about to do.

Seconds later, Miles's security team had swooped in and were doing their best to get both of us back on our feet and Ollie as far away from us as possible.

"So sorry, old chap," Ollie said to Miles, looking embarrassed as he backed away.

"You ripped my dress," I said, horrified, looking down at my outfit.

"Truly sorry," Ollie repeated. Then he began to move back toward us as if he intended to help fix the fake tear I'd just made up. "Here, let me just help . . ."

I stepped away and put my hands up in front of me to stop him.

"No, don't," I said forcefully. "You've done *enough*."

"Don't go—" Miles began, trying to come up with an excuse to make me stay.

But I was finished there.

"I'm sorry," I said, placing my hand on his arm lightly to reassure him. "I'll just go . . . fix myself up. The fundraiser needs you. I'll be fine."

And then I turned around and sped off toward the main house to find a bathroom as Miles stood there, openmouthed, watching me leave.

Once I was inside, I headed straight for the first bathroom I could find. As luck would have it, somebody was on their way out as I showed up, so I brushed past him and locked the door behind me.

Inside the guest bathroom were a chaise lounge in one corner and a lit-up vanity against one of the far walls. I skipped the toilet and sink and went right over to the vanity and sat down on the tufted chair in front of it. I studied myself in the mirror. A few feathers were out of place, but besides that, I didn't look any the worse for wear.

I smiled as I thought back to the scene we'd made minutes before. I had to hand it to him, Ollie had really put on a show. In fact, the whole thing had been better than when we'd rehearsed.

Ollie had been a natural.

My thoughts were interrupted by a knock at the door.

"Someone's in here!" I called out, hoping the person would just go away.

But then the knock came again, and I sighed.

"I said—" I began before I was cut off.

"It's me," I heard Ollie whisper loudly through the door, still in his British accent.

Standing up from the seat, I rushed over to the door and opened it just wide enough for him to slip inside.

"How did I do?" he asked, looking concerned.

"Well, I think you officially pissed Miles off," I said.

"Darn," Ollie said with fake sincerity. "And I was hoping we'd be friends. Did you get it?"

A slow smile emerged on my face as I shoved my hands into the pocket of my dress and pulled out the cell phone I'd stolen from inside Miles's jacket.

"But of course, dear chap," I answered in my own fake British accent, and held it up for him to see.

Entry Thirty-Four

I turned the phone over in my hands and found the smarmy billionaire staring back at me, his smile glowing white and his face wrinkle-free. I cringed as I remembered him flirting with me and fought the urge to smash the jeweled smile off his face.

Instead, I ran my fingers across the precious diamonds that made up the picture and held the phone up to study it closer.

It looked exactly like the one I'd replaced it with. Only, this one was real, while the other was not.

"Yowza," Ollie said as the diamonds shimmered in the bathroom light. "Definitely an upgrade from my phone."

"Yeah, but yours doesn't make me want to gag," I said, turning it off so we couldn't be tracked.

"So what next?" Ollie asked as I reached back into my pocket and started pulling things out and placing them in front of us.

A roll of tape.

A compact of loose face powder and a makeup brush.

A pair of latex gloves.

"I need Miles's fingerprint to get into his treasure room," I said.

"And we're going to get that by . . . putting on makeup?" he asked, watching me curiously.

"Beauty is key," I responded, snapping each of the gloves as I secured them on my hands.

I picked up the compact and dipped the makeup brush into it gently. I held the brush up for Ollie to see before blowing the excess powder into his face jokingly.

As he sputtered, I leaned back down and lightly ran the brush and powder over the screen of Miles's iPhone until it was covered. With another gentle blow, the excess powder flew away, leaving a bunch of smudged prints.

All except for . . . bingo!

There was one perfect thumbprint.

Grabbing the tape dispenser and ripping a piece off, I carefully lowered it onto the now-visible print. With a slight tap of my finger, the sticky side of the tape did its work, and I stood back up with a perfect duplicate of Miles's thumbprint.

"So cool," Ollie said, squinting at the final product.

"Right?" I said. "Who knew makeup could be so useful?"

I took another piece of tape and enclosed the print so it wouldn't smudge before I could use it. Then I placed it back in my pocket.

Finally I pulled off the gloves and picked up the compact, displaying both to Ollie like a magician showing off for his audience. Then, with more flourish than was needed, I dumped the rest of the powder inside one of the gloves and tied it off in a knot at the top.

"What's that for?" Ollie asked, looking confused as I shoved the empty compact and brush back into my pocket along with the tape dispenser and the single empty glove.

I could've tossed it all in the trash, but you never leave behind evidence of any kind. Much safer to dispose of it all later, when it can't be tied back to the crime.

"Most people think a print is all you need to pass a finger-print ID, but they're wrong," I explained. "What people don't realize is that the fingerprint-recognition technology wants more than that. It wants the *finger,* too."

I held the latex glove up to show him that when it was filled with the powder, it resembled a real live hand.

"The scanner would know if we just put the piece of tape down with the print. It's smart. It would know there was no finger backing it up," I said. "But attach the fin-gerprint to this . . ."

I placed the piece of tape with Miles's fingerprint on it on top of the thumb of the glove and held it up for Ollie to see.

". . . and suddenly you've got what will pass as the hand that the fingerprint belongs to."

Ollie gave me an impressed look and started to clap slowly.

"This is why you're the master," he joked, bowing to me grandly.

I curtsied in response before placing the powder-filled glove in my other pocket.

"Okay, wish me luck," I said, giving him a smile as I reached for the bathroom door. "I've got a secret room to break into."

Entry Thirty-Five

As I snuck off to break into Miles's man cave, Ollie wandered back to the party. The next part of our plan had him keeping an eye on Miles to make sure he didn't come back into the house while I was robbing him blind.

Smoothing down the feathers of my dress, I sauntered past the guests mingling in Miles's living room and disappeared down the hallway I knew led to the office. As soon as I was out of sight, I pressed the button on my surveillance scrambler so my whereabouts from there on out couldn't be traced. When the hallway veered off to the right, I followed it, knowing that Miles's office was just ten feet beyond.

Unfortunately, so was another of Miles's security team. He spotted me right away and unfolded his arms as I approached.

"Um, is someone supposed to be retching into the crystal vase out there?" I asked him wide-eyed, pointing behind me.

As soon as I said it, the guy took off past me to take care of the supposed incident.

And as I'd hoped, he'd left me alone outside Miles's office.

Rushing over to the door, I paused, looking over my shoulder one last time before slipping inside.

As I pulled the door shut behind me, I was enveloped in darkness. I blinked in an attempt to help my eyes adjust but gave up after a few seconds and pulled out the tiny penlight I'd stashed away for just such an occasion.

The light was small enough that it wouldn't alert anyone outside that I was in there, but it would at least get me across the room and over to Miles's desk without running into anything.

I pulled out Miles's leather chair and tried to sit down in the poufy dress, but after a few attempts, I just kicked the chair away behind me. I heard it hit the far wall with a tiny clang and grimaced at my bad judgment.

When nobody came rushing into the room to investigate the noise, I got to work pulling out everything I'd need to get into Miles's treasure room.

I laid each item side by side like a doctor does her tools before surgery. There was something about the act of getting everything in order that was oddly calming.

The latex glove.

Miles's fingerprint.

A little black recorder.

I picked up the recorder and turned the volume as low as I could get it before holding it up to my ear. When I pressed Play, the voices began to flow out immediately and I smiled.

"You should really consider starting your own foundation, you know?" My voice came out strong and slightly flirty. "The Christian Miles Foundation, maybe? I could be your first supporter."

"I like that. *The Christian Miles Foundation,*" Miles's voice responded loud and clear.

I pressed Rewind and played it again.

"I like that. The—"

I pressed Pause and laid the recorder back down on the desk next to the other items.

Now I was ready.

Reaching up under Miles's desk, I found the button that opened the control panel and pressed it.

A quiet whirring filled the room as the desk spread apart to reveal the speaker and tiny square of black glass.

Almost immediately, the computerized British woman's voice called out, "Prepare voice recognition and fingerprint scan."

The sound was louder than I remembered it being. Then again, there was far more at stake tonight than there had been the first time I'd been in Miles's office.

I froze in place and looked at the door for some sign that Miles's security detail was going to burst in at any moment. But all was quiet.

At least for now.

As the British computer lady began to talk again, I pulled the recorder over and pressed Play as I held it down to the speaker.

"Christian Miles."

Miles's voice rang out of the recorder and I paused it before it could continue.

"Voice recognition accepted," the British woman said. "Commence fingerprint scan now."

"Shhhh," I begged the recording as she bellowed out her commands.

I took the latex glove, positioned Miles's taped print on the thumb, and placed them down on the square glass.

"Fingerprint not recognized," the British computer's voice called out.

Oh, no.

My stomach dropped.

Swallowing hard, I picked the glove up and straightened it before placing it back on the scanner over the taped print.

"Fingerprint not recognized," the British computer lady repeated.

"Come on, come on, come on!" I whispered, picking the glove up one last time and forcing the finger more into a thumb shape before placing it lightly on the glass below.

And then I held my breath and waited.

One second.

Two seconds.

Three seconds.

"Fingerprint accepted," the British computer finally chirped out into the darkness as more whirring began and the desk began to move underneath my hands.

My adrenaline began to surge as I watched the floor open up and reveal a tiny staircase leading down into darkness. When the desk finally stopped moving, I grabbed my tools and began to walk slowly down the steps, only the penlight lighting my way.

I shivered as I began to descend. It was colder down here. Like walking into a basement. Only, I could feel that it was air conditioning that was regulating the temperature and not that I was in some dank, dark cave. That at least gave me some comfort. Because usually, walking down into dark, hidden places isn't my idea of a good time.

And for all I knew, I could be walking into Miles's super-creepy, super-secret dungeon. The one where he literally kept all his skeletons.

At this thought, I hesitated, wondering for the first time if this was a good idea.

But then lights began to flash on around me, illuminating the darkness and showcasing a clean, sleek room.

"Not bad," I said, looking around Miles's hidden treasure room in awe.

As I walked toward the middle of the space, I heard the desk in the office above begin to slide back into place. Most people would probably freak at the thought of being locked in a room they weren't yet sure how to get out of, but at this particular moment, I didn't care. If there was a way in, there was a way out. And for now, I definitely wanted to be in here.

Because this was where Miles was hiding his most valuable loot.

He'd divided the room up into sections, sort of like his own mini museum. On one wall he'd hung several pieces of art. As I got close to them, I could read the golden plaques affixed to the frames.

HENRI MATISSE

PIERRE-AUGUSTE RENOIR

PAUL CÉZANNE

JACKSON POLLOCK

All the greats were there. The question was, why? Most art collectors display their purchases where anyone can see them, eager to show off both their supposed good taste and their abundant wealth.

But these? These were hidden away where only Miles could enjoy them.

I studied the painting closest to me. It looked like a watercolor of a countryside, lush green hills surrounding some sort of building or cluster of houses. It was perfectly nice, but nothing special if you asked me.

The plaque read *View of Auvers-sur-Oise by Paul Cézanne*.

Curious why it had made it into Miles's hidden room, I Googled the title from the burner phone and very quickly found out why.

The painting in front of me was stolen. Presumed to be

taken from the Ashmolean Museum in Oxford, England, back in 1999 during a celebration of fireworks put on the night before the millennium.

Its estimated worth? Ten million dollars.

Quick searches of the other paintings hanging on Miles's wall showed the same situation. All extremely valuable. All extremely stolen or presumed missing.

I shook my head.

There's a reason thieves don't steal famous art. And this was it. Most thieves steal with the ultimate goal of making money. Sure, sometimes it's for fun, or for the challenge of taking the unattainable. But that's not what keeps us going.

What keeps us going is money.

And that means that whatever we steal, we have to be able to resell.

Famous art is nearly impossible to resell.

This is because the people who really want it—the ones who would pay an insane amount of money to own a piece—want to display it. Whether it's in a museum or a personal gallery in their home, the reason a person would spend $50 million on a van Gogh is to show it off.

And if it's stolen? Well, you can't exactly brag about that. Or, you could, but you'd get caught and the painting would go back to whoever it belonged to anyway, so what's the point?

I had no idea why Miles would have stolen art. It didn't make any sense, but then again a lot of what he did didn't make sense to me. One thing was sure, though . . . I wouldn't be leaving here with any of it.

Same went for the statues and sculptures he had placed around the room. After looking one up and finding that it had been mysteriously taken from its owner over a century before, I decided those were lost causes too.

I was beginning to think I'd have to walk away from Miles's treasure room with nothing to help the people he'd swindled at the apartment complex he owned. And the thought was more than disappointing.

It was downright unacceptable.

There *had* to be something down there that I could take and turn into money for those who'd been cheated by Miles.

There just had to be.

That's when I remembered it. The money that was supposedly hidden on Miles's property. What better place to hide it than in this secret, locked room?

I began to pull pictures away from the wall and other stuff down off its hinges.

And there, behind an ugly framed photo of Christian Miles and President Trump, was the outside of a safe.

Entry Thirty-Six

"Jackpot," I whispered, rubbing my hands together excitedly.

The safe wasn't anything special. Just your regular, run-of-the-mill wall safe. Certainly not one that could keep a seasoned thief like me out.

In fact, getting it open was going to be pretty simple. People don't realize how easy it is to open most safes.

Of course, the ones in banks or museums or casinos are much more state-of-the-art. They have fail-safes upon fail-safes, multiple alarms, shutdown mechanisms—you name it, those kinds of places have them.

But home safes? Well, in thieves' circles, they're known as expensive cabinets. Might as well leave them wide open for as much as they do to keep people like me and my dad out.

Still, I appreciate the fact that rich people believe safes are enough to keep their valuables safe.

It makes my job easier.

Digging into another hidden pocket that Ollie had somehow managed to sew into my costume, I pulled out a small velvet drawstring bag. Inside was a wooden box about the size of a jewelry store bracelet container. I opened it up, pulled out a round, hockey-puck-sized magnet, and held it up in the light.

It was a rare-earth magnet, and it's been part of my tool kit for more than five years now. It was actually one of the first pieces Dad gave me and has come in handy more often than you'd expect a magnet to.

Because a rare-earth magnet like the one I was holding can open pretty much anything. A hotel room. An apartment complex. An unmarked entrance leading into a military bunker.

And especially a safe.

I slipped the magnet into an old tube sock and took it over to the safe. Then, slowly placing it against the front surface, I moved it around until the magnet found the nickel piece inside the safe. Once I felt the connection, I simply dragged the magnet to the left and pulled down on the lever to open it.

"Easy peasy," I said with a smile as I let the door swing wide.

And then I looked inside.

In all the articles I'd read about Miles and his secret treasure room, it had been rumored that he kept up to a million dollars in a secret safe somewhere on the property.

All these articles had been wrong.

Because I could see that there was way more than a million in there. It was probably more like three to four times that amount, actually.

And it was all there for the taking.

Grabbing one of the closest stacks, I fanned through it like a deck of cards, estimating that there were fifty bills in each stack. And each of the bills was marked with a great big green 100 on it.

"Holy—" I started to say as I worked out in my head just how much money I was looking at.

Then I promptly began to pull out stacks upon stacks of the money, until the floor at my feet was covered. I thought briefly about what it would be like to take the bundles apart and throw them into the air while watching the money fall down around me. But the point was to leave the place looking like I'd never been there.

No, I would have to make it rain later.

Instead, I lifted up the side of my dress, revealing a hole in the seam near the waist, and began shoving the stacks inside.

This was the actual genius of the outfit. Ollie had built this whole area underneath the skirt where I could hide just about anything. As soon as I dropped it into the hole in the seam, the item—in this case, a stack of five grand—would fall down into the sacklike structure built around the crinoline.

It was kind of incredible if you thought about it. The pouf of the raven's tail made it impossible to see that I had anything hidden under there. Which meant I would be able to sneak out of the party completely undetected.

But just to be clear, I didn't take it all.

I didn't really need to, and the smarter thing would be to leave at least half of it so that it wouldn't be immediately noticeable that the money had been stolen.

The most successful robberies are the ones that nobody ever finds out about. And that means no cops to come looking for you.

So when I was finished grabbing the amount I wanted, I pulled the cash that was in the back toward the front, pried the magnet from the safe, and closed it, hearing it lock back up on its own.

I could've left right then. And maybe I should've. I'd gotten more than what I'd gone there for and the rest of the stuff would've been impossible to resell on any market.

But something held me back.

Something inside me was screaming that there was more in there for me. Something that was worth more than anything I'd already found. Call it a hunch. Or maybe some weird intuition.

But I'd learned to trust my gut. And my gut was telling me not to leave just yet.

So I stopped in the middle of the room and took another look around.

At first, nothing jumped out at me. But as I took another sweep, I finally saw it.

There was a row of surveillance screens hanging on the far wall. I'd noticed them almost as soon as I'd entered the room but hadn't given it a second thought since they weren't recording me. I'd been focused mostly on finding Miles's valuables. And it's not unusual for a homeowner like Miles to have his own security cameras to watch what's going on in his own home. Makes him feel like the master of his castle. Like he's in control.

But cameras also have another purpose.

They allow the person watching to catch people in moments they intended to be private. Moments they don't necessarily want other people to witness. And certainly don't intend to have recorded.

Walking over to the wall of screens slowly, I looked at each one before finding the one I wanted.

Miles's office.

The one situated right above me.

The control panel was built into the wall right below the screens, and I immediately began to fiddle with it, calling up Miles's office and then rewinding as far as it would go.

I wasn't totally sure what I was looking for, but I hurried through the recording anyway, stopping to play it back whenever I saw Miles in the room with someone or on the phone.

Most of it wasn't helpful. Just a bunch of boring stuff about the real estate business or Miles talking about how important he thought he was.

But then I saw something that made my heart speed up and frantically pressed Play.

It was dated a few weeks ago. Without thinking about it, I pulled out my phone and started to record what I was seeing.

On the screen, Miles had just entered his office, followed by the sketchy lawyer I'd seen in court that day with Uncle Scotty. They were making small talk at first. Miles asked the lawyer how his flight on the private jet had been. The lawyer said it had been fine and added some sleaze-baggy comment about the hotness of the stewardess.

But then the conversation shifted.

On the video, Miles walked over to the bar near his desk and poured himself a few inches of a brown liquid before walking back to his couch and sitting down.

"So where are we on this lawsuit with the broad from the south side?" Miles asked, taking a sip of his drink.

"It's not going to hold," the lawyer said, standing in front of his boss. You could tell he'd rather have been sitting, but since Miles hadn't offered him a seat, he was stuck on his feet. "There's no evidence that Mrs. Martinez ever asked for anything to be fixed, and without that, they've got nothing."

"And you're sure they can't track down those 'missing requests'?" Miles asked, using air quotes.

"Mr. Miles, we hired the best people in the world to create that site for you," the lawyer reassured him. "They've guaranteed us that requests will disappear as soon as they're made. There is no way that Mrs. Martinez can prove her case without those requests."

"Good," Miles said, nodding thoughtfully. After a moment, he looked back up at the lawyer and gave him a nasty smile. "Still, I think it would be worth reaching out to Judge Meyer. Remind him that we've been quiet about that incident of his in Cabo so far, but we might just find ourselves having a crisis of conscience in the future if this doesn't go our way."

"Of course," the lawyer said, nodding as he took out his phone and typed furiously on it for a few seconds.

"Tell me again why we can't just make these people . . . *disappear*? Like the others?" Miles asked, waving his hand in the air languidly.

"That may have worked for them, but Mrs. Martinez isn't illegal," the lawyer explained, as if this wasn't his first time telling Miles this.

"She's not exactly *American*, though, either?" Miles said, snorting. He threw the rest of his drink back and stood up, walking over to the bar for another one.

"I promise we'll make this go away in court," the lawyer said, clearly not wanting to argue with a guy like Miles.

"You better," Miles answered, not quite threatening him. It was more a matter-of-fact. "Just remember, I always get what I want."

"Of course, sir," the lawyer said. "That's what I'm here for."

As I watched the lawyer leave Miles alone in the room, I paused the video and stopped recording.

"That dirty, swindling mouth-breather," I said angrily.

I turned around to survey the room again and narrowed my eyes as I had another idea. Flipping my phone back toward the walls of Miles's secret treasure room, I pressed Record.

"You're not getting what you want this time," I muttered, and began to record everything I saw.

• • •

Five minutes later, I was headed back up the stairs after the floor automatically opened, and emerged from the hidden entrance beneath Miles's desk. What little light had been shining behind me disappeared as the floor closed back up and Miles's desk slipped back into place, leaving me once again in total darkness.

By now, though, I had a feel for the layout of his office and knew that all I needed to do was make my way around the desk and then it was a straight shot to the door.

Ready to get out of there, I quickened my pace until I could feel the presence of the door in front of me. I stopped for just a second to listen for anyone who might be on the other side, but all I could hear was the typical noise of the party in the distance.

Taking a deep breath, I grabbed hold of the door handle and pulled it open.

"And where are you coming from?" a deep voice asked as soon as I'd taken a step out into the hallway.

My head jerked to the left as my gaze fell on another security guard. This one was different from the one I'd sent away earlier, but like the other, he was leaning up against the wall, his massive arms folded in front of him.

And he was not happy to see me.

Swallowing hard, I pulled the door to Miles's office closed behind me and looked in the opposite direction for

some way of escaping. I knew I wouldn't be able to out-
run the guard. Not in the dress and heels I was wearing.
And not weighted down with as much cash as I currently
had on me.

I'd have to come up with something else.

So, thinking quickly, I turned to the guard and placed
my hands on my hips defiantly.

"Where is your boss?" I hissed. "Miles told me to join
him here for a private . . . *meeting*. And well, as you can
see, he never showed up! I have never been so insulted in
my life."

I let my voice grow into a growl as I walked toward
the man, wagging my finger at him like he was the one I
was angry at. His eyes widened as I stepped closer to him,
and he dropped his arms to his side like he wasn't sure
how to handle the situation.

So I pushed even further, walking right up to him and
poking him in the chest.

"You tell that *jerk* Miles that *nobody* keeps Lola
Lafonta waiting," I said threateningly. Then I spun
around on my heel and began to strut off toward the rest
of the party before throwing behind me, "Nobody!"

I added this last bit just as I was disappearing around
the corner, and then I booked it toward the exit, hoping
the security guy wasn't following me.

Just as I reached the front door, I heard someone call
out, "Wait!"

I almost froze where I stood, sure the security guard

was after me, but when I turned my head, I saw Ollie just a few steps behind me. He already looked out of breath but motioned for me to keep going anyway.

Once we were outside, we began the long walk down the driveway to where we'd eventually call a cab and finally make our escape.

We'd barely gone a few feet before Ollie turned to me with a smile and said, "I just want to know one thing."

"Don't worry, I got it," I said, patting the tail of my dress. "I got it all."

Ollie smiled but shook his head. "That's great, but it's not what I was going to ask."

I glanced at him, confused. "Then what?"

After a pause, he finally said, "What's escargot?"

I immediately began to laugh, which made him frown.

"Hey, it was fried and it looked like calamari, so I took a bite," he explained as we walked. "And it wasn't so bad. So I had some more. But then I remembered all that other weird food and got worried. . . ."

I laughed again, this time even louder.

"What? What did I eat, Frankie?" he pleaded, looking like he was going to be sick. "Just tell me."

I put my arm around my friend as we walked through the darkness together.

"I think it's better that you don't know," I said finally, then clapped him on his back before running off ahead of him, laughing, into the night.

Entry Thirty-Seven

"So there was *nothing* in Miles's treasure room that you could steal?" Ollie asked, sounding slightly disappointed.

"I wouldn't exactly call one-point-six million dollars nothing, Ollie," I said quietly as we walked down the loud hallway to the lunchroom.

We hadn't had much time to go over the ultimate outcome of the heist at Miles's. Not between trying to escape the estate without being caught, and then being stuck with a cabbie who refused to turn on the radio, forcing us to drive the whole way home in silence. And then it had been the weekend, which meant family time with Uncle Scotty and a whole lot of phone calls to put a few things into motion on my end.

At least Ollie knew the operation had gone well. But once again we had to catch up on the details at school.

Not exactly ideal, but I was starting to get used to sneaking around with Ollie and having our top secret conversations out in public. It was almost like a challenge. How far could we push those boundaries without anyone else being the wiser?

"Point taken, Richie Rich," Ollie said. "So what are you doing with the money?"

"You mean *our* money?" I asked, raising my eyebrow. "You were there too. That means you get a cut."

"Nah, I didn't do this for the Benjamins," Ollie said, shaking his head. "I did it the same reason you did it. The guy's a scumbag and I wanted to help. Besides, who needs—how much would my cut have been?"

"About eight hundred thousand," I answered.

Ollie just about choked on the gum he was chewing as I said this, but then coughed a few times before regaining his breath.

"Right," he said again. "Who needs that kind of money anyway? Not me."

He said it like it pained him just a little, but I could tell deep down that he didn't care about the cash.

"I was hoping you'd say that," I said, giving him a shy smile. "Because I've already spent a lot of it."

Ollie's head shot over as he looked at me.

"Are you serious?" he asked. "It's been two days! How did you burn through that much so quickly?"

"I'm about to show you," I said, and I steered him over to the lunch table where Ryan and the rest of his friends were sitting.

"Hey, guys!" Ollie said as he shot a questioning glance my way before sitting down. I followed suit and then opened up a bag of Red Vines before offering some to the table. "What's going on?"

"Ollie, man, you won't believe what happened!" Ryan

said almost immediately. He'd been talking animatedly to the other kids at the table when we'd walked up and still seemed ready to burst with excitement. "They're fixing everything. And I mean Every. Little. Thing."

"Wait. They're fixing what exactly?" Ollie asked, confused.

I just sat there chewing on my licorice, my face a complete blank.

"Everything," Ryan said, shaking his head like he couldn't believe it. "At our apartment. These worker guys showed up this weekend—like, all over the whole Southside complex—and they just started fixing everything. No more rats, no more holes in the walls, no more crappy places to live."

"You don't say?" Ollie said, sneaking a glance over at me. I refused to look at him.

"And that's not all. There's all this new stuff, too. Like fridges, and stoves and heaters and washers," Ryan said, ticking the stuff off on his fingers. "Dude, we don't have to go to the laundromat anymore to do our laundry, because it's *right there,* in the complex!"

"That's awesome, man!" Ollie said, grinning as he stole a Red Vine from me and took a big bite.

"My dad says Miles must've finally come to his senses and decided to fix it all," Ryan said, thinking long and hard about this. "But I think it was something else. *Someone* else maybe?"

This time I could feel Ryan's eyes pan over to me. I managed to keep my face neutral, but I didn't look him in the eye. He might've been onto me.

"Why do you think someone else was involved?" Ollie asked, not as good as I was at keeping a straight face. I kicked him under the table and willed him to be cool. "I mean, it sounds like what you said. That Miles guy just stopped being a punk."

"Yeah, maybe," Ryan said, not sounding convinced. "But there's something else."

At this, Ryan leaned toward the two of us like he didn't want the others to hear what he was about to say.

"Someone left us . . . *money*," he whispered. "And a lot of it. Enough for us to pay our rent this month and next. My dad talked to the neighbors and the same thing happened to them. I wasn't supposed to know about it, but I overheard my parents talking, and they think it's, like, hush money or something."

"Hush money for what?" Ollie asked.

"I don't know. Maybe because the place was such a dump," Ryan said with a shrug. Then he turned to me. "Didn't you say that lady Mrs. Martinez just took Miles to court? Maybe this is all because of her."

I shook my head. "I don't know," I said. "She actually lost the case."

"Oh," Ryan said, sounding surprised.

"Does it matter where it's all coming from, though?"

Ollie asked him finally. "Like, isn't it just cool that it's happening?"

"Sure. Of course," Ryan said, his eyes growing big. "Don't get me wrong, I'm not complaining. I think I'm just wondering . . . like, who to thank?"

Without looking at him directly, I said slowly, "Maybe there's nobody to thank. Maybe it's just the universe's way of working things out. Karma and all that."

Ryan thought about this as he took a bite of his sandwich.

"Yeah," he said. "Maybe."

After a few seconds of silence, I placed my hands on the table and stood up.

"We should go get food before the jocks take all the good stuff," I said to Ollie.

"Right," Ollie said, his head snapping over to me at the mention of food. "I've been craving a few taco boats myself. See you, man."

"See you," Ryan said, still looking at me curiously.

"So *that's* where the money went?" Ollie asked once we were far enough away from Ryan's table.

I just nodded. "It was the right thing to do," I said. "I'm also setting up anonymous college funds in the names of all the kids who've lived there while Miles has been on his reign of terror."

Ollie let out a low whistle. "But how long can you really keep that up, Frankie?" he asked. "The money we got *sounds* like a lot, but it's not gonna last much longer."

"You're right," I said as we walked to the lunch counter and joined the back of the line. "It won't."

"Well then, is that it, then?" Ollie asked. He didn't sound accusatory. I knew Ollie thought that what we'd done so far was enough. It was more like, he knew *me*. And he knew I'd never leave it at just that.

"Nope," I said. And then I paused for dramatic effect. "You know, I *did* leave Miles's with something other than the money. A few other things, actually."

Ollie turned to me in surprise.

"I thought that was all you got," he said.

"I said I didn't take anything of his from the treasure room except for the money," I corrected him. "I didn't say the money was all I got."

"You sneaky little minx," Ollie said. "So what *did* you get? Please tell me it was one of his cars."

I gave him a look and rolled my eyes. "When would I have gotten one of his cars?" I asked. "We took a cab home, you goof."

"Oh, right," he said. "Well then, what?"

"This," I said, and pulled out my cell phone. Going into my videos, I found the one of Miles admitting he'd messed with Mrs. Martinez's case and handed it over for Ollie to watch. "I have a feeling this video will thoroughly ruin Christian Miles's reputation when people see it. And they *will* see it. Probably later this afternoon, I'd guess. The video file was sent to New York's three biggest newspapers this morning by 'an anonymous source.' Oh, and if that doesn't totally screw up his life, I also sent the video of all the illegal paintings and sculptures he's got hiding in his secret room to Uncle Scotty's work."

"You're devious!" Ollie said, though the grin on his face told me he thought it was amazing.

We ordered our food and waited as the people working behind the counter got our meals together. I was starved by all this do-gooder stuff and didn't even wait to sit down before starting to pop fries into my mouth.

"You're still gonna run out of money soon, though, Frankie," Ollie said as we walked back to the lunch tables. "You know that, right? I mean, I love what you were trying to do and you've probably already changed these people's lives more than you know. But the money isn't going to last much longer."

"I still haven't told you the last thing we snagged from Miles," I said, chewing on a French fry mysteriously.

"I'm listening," Ollie said.

"You know how the plan was supposed to be to switch Miles's phone back at the end of the night? Take the duplicate with us?" I said slowly. "Well . . . I didn't."

"You *kept* it?" Ollie asked, his voice getting all high and squeaky.

"I did," I said, nodding.

"I thought you hated that thing," he said, clearly remembering how I'd wanted to smash the picture of Miles into a million little pieces the night of the gala.

"I did," I said. "Until I Googled it while I was in the treasure room and found out that it's worth *sixteen million dollars.*"

Ollie started to choke and I had to smack him on the back to make sure he was okay.

"Sixteen million dollars for that thing?" he asked incredulously.

"It was covered in gold and diamonds. Hundreds of them," I explained. "Rare, too. And completely untraceable. Which means . . ."

"Which means you can sell off all the parts," Ollie deduced, shaking his head.

"I've got a guy," I said, winking at him. "So what do you think? Does that cover all the people in Ryan's apartment complex or what?"

"I would say so," Ollie said with a laugh.

I pointed to a table that was free over in the corner and Ollie and I made our way toward it. Ollie was in the lead, winding through the throngs of other students eating their lunches, and I was trailing behind, still thinking about everything we'd accomplished in the span of a few weeks.

And I was so distracted that I almost didn't see it coming.

Ollie had just passed by a table full of girls, and as soon as his back was to them, one of them stood up and began to follow him, her tray held high—and full.

It dawned on me almost immediately what was about to happen and something inside me snapped. Without thinking about the consequences, I sprinted forward, and just as the tray began to tip down toward Ollie's head, I flipped it in the opposite direction.

Right on top of the girl's head.

Ketchup, milk shake, leftover fries, and various other remnants of the girl's lunch cascaded down the front of her, leaving her a gooey mess.

And that's when she began to scream.

It was louder than I thought possible, and it immediately made everyone in the cafeteria turn and look at her.

I was still standing there, just inches away from the girl, when she slowly turned around to look at me, a murderous look in her eyes.

"Annabelle," I said, only slightly surprised when I realized who it was. Though I really shouldn't have been. Nobody else would've been so evil that she would've purposely tried to tray someone like Ollie.

"You little freak!" she screamed at me. "What's your problem?"

Everyone in the room heard this, too, of course. Because the whole place had gone silent as soon as they'd seen what was happening.

And there wasn't a single person who wasn't currently staring at the two of us. I looked just past Annabelle's shoulder and saw that Ollie had turned and was staring at us, too. I couldn't quite place the look on his face, but it was obvious he knew what had happened. Or what Annabelle had tried to make happen.

But all anyone else in the school knew was that Annabelle was covered in, well, lunch. And it appeared like I was the one who'd done it to her.

Needless to say, it was way more attention than I'd ever wanted to have on me and I froze as I thought quickly through my options.

I could apologize profusely and rush to get napkins to help Annabelle clean up. I would still be able to keep my cover if everyone thought it had just been a mistake and I was really *that* clumsy.

I could run away and hope people would be so focused on helping Annabelle that they'd forget all about me.

I looked over at Ollie again and watched as he put down his tray and began to walk back toward us. At first I wanted to ask him what he was doing, but then it clicked. He was coming back because he had *my* back.

He wasn't going to make me deal with this on my own, because he was my friend.

My best friend.

And in that instant, I knew I was going to go with option three.

I could stop thinking only of myself for a minute and stand up to the bullies who were trying to make my friend's life miserable.

So that's what I did.

"What's my problem, Annabelle? That would be *you*," I said clearly.

Because it was still so silent around us, the words came out much more loudly than I'd intended. Still, I didn't quiet my voice. I needed it to come out strong. I needed her to hear me and know I wasn't kidding. I needed Ollie to understand that our friendship wasn't one-sided. That I would *always* stand up for him. After all, I'd just helped a bunch of strangers when they'd needed someone. It was time for me to help my best friend, too.

"I know that other people around here have let you pull this kind of crap on them, but I'm telling you now, it's *going to stop*," I said, taking a step closer so she was forced to look me straight in the eye. "I don't care if you hate me. I don't care if you say things about me behind my back. But you do *not* get to mess with my friends. Because if you do . . . well, I think you know what will happen. Understand?"

Annabelle just stared at me, her mouth hanging open like a fish out of water. I waited for her to say something back to me, but the nasty retort didn't come. Instead, someone in the room started to clap.

And then another person joined in, and another, until the whole place had erupted in applause.

With one last glance at the mutiny around her, Annabelle finally stalked off toward the bathroom, her friends following close behind, heads all tilted toward the ground.

I took a deep breath and then, without looking at anyone else, caught up to Ollie, and we walked outside together.

"That was better than the series finale of *Game of Thrones*," Ollie breathed once we were a decent distance away from the school.

I just looked at him and rolled my eyes.

"You know you didn't have to do that," he said, suddenly serious. "They're gonna make you their target from now on."

"I *did* have to do it, Ollie," I said, stopping midstep and turning to face him. "I couldn't let them do that to you. It wasn't right. And it wouldn't have been right if I'd stood by and let it happen. Ollie, you're my—"

Ugh, the moment was bordering on an after-school special and I really didn't want to have to admit out loud all this mushy gushy stuff. So I stopped.

"Frankie Lorde, are you trying to say that I'm . . . your *best friend*?"

"I didn't say that," I argued, already feeling annoyed by the smile that had erupted on his face.

"Admit it, you're *obsessed* with me," Ollie said teasingly. "You want to have slumber parties and talk about boys and make BFF bracelets—"

"You are such a dork!" I screamed, but I'd already begun to laugh.

We started to walk again, this time in silence. But after a few steps, Ollie cleared his throat, and I looked at him.

"So what's the next job?" he asked, a smile playing on his lips.

"Well, Ollie," I answered. "I'm glad you asked. . . ."

Acknowledgments

I feel like a lot of things had to align perfectly in the universe to make this book happen. First and foremost, I have to thank Bethany Buck, editor extraordinaire, for falling in love with Frankie before I'd even named her, and for seeing the potential in both me and the book. The experience of writing this with you has truly been a delight and privilege. Thanks to my marvelous agent Reiko Davis for taking a chance on me when nobody else would. I feel so lucky to have you in my corner.

Kristin Bell and Rob Thomas . . . thank you for inspiring me to create badass female characters who are complicated, funny, daring, and marshmallowy. I like to think there's a little bit of Veronica Mars in Frankie.

To my friends: Colleen, thank you for all the inside knowledge you gave me on Greenwich. You couldn't have been a better tour guide and friend. And Sailor, you're the coolest middle schooler around. To all the mommies at Discovery, thank you for your friendship and smiles as we trudge this road called motherhood together. Frack, nobody was happier or more excited for me than you were when I got this book deal. You'll always be my soul sister. Mary Rose, thank you for your encouragement when I wasn't feeling very creative and for helping me to come up with appropriate put-downs for my characters. You're such a jerk face. Natasha, our friendship has been fast and furious, but you've already proven to be one of my most loyal confidants. Lastly, Mikey and Lauren, you guys have been there for me through the good times and bad. There's no one tougher, lovelier, smarter, or funnier than you two. You've been my lifelines. Mamma's for life!

Andrea, thanks for always treating me like your daughter and for helping me brainstorm titles for this book. Price, I appreciate the legal advice you gave me while writing my courtroom scene . . . even if I *did* end up taking some fictional liberties.

Mom and Dad, thanks for all your love and support, and for always encouraging me to follow my passion. I'll try to keep making you proud. After all . . . I *am* your favorite.

Jacey, thank you for continuing to be my #1 fan and inspiring me every day just by being you.

To the rest of my family who've always had my back: Amy, Cody, Cash, Riley, Katy, Ryan, Robin, River, Oma, Aunt Marsha, Uncle Mike, Aunt Mary, Chelle, Maya, Daniel, Dan, Karin, Michael, Justin, Julia, James, Kelly, Tommy, Lily, Laney, Andrew, Billy, Auntie Anne, Aunt Denise, Aunt Mary Ellen, Aunt Mary, Uncle Nick, and Aunt Claudette. I'm grateful for each and every one of you.

Kayla, I *literally* couldn't have written or edited this

book without you around. Thank you for letting me talk your ear off about Frankie and her adventures, and for being one of the first people to read the finished book.

Huck, thanks for keeping yourself occupied and not destroying the house (too much), while mommy was writing this book. You're my favorite troublemaker. Grey, your brother never let me write while I was pregnant with him. Thank you for being more agreeable and allowing me to keep hold of some of my energy while you were growing in my belly, so I could also bring Frankie to life. You're such a cool character!

Finally, Matt, thank you for introducing me to Pixel+Ink and making this all possible in the first place. Also, for continuing to believe in me so much that you don't mind bringing home the bacon so that I can spend my days making up stories. You're my ultimate partner in crime.

Ever since she and Ollie took down Christian Miles, Frankie's been itching to find her next mark . . .

And she might've just found it. While volunteering at a local animal shelter over winter break, Frankie and Ollie get word that there's a dangerous exotic-animal farm supplying Greenwich's elite with lions and tigers and bears (oh no!).

Feeling an instant kinship with the endangered creatures locked away in their cages, Frankie makes it her mission to find the perpetrators, free the beautiful beasts, and ensnare the bad guys in a trap of her own.

Now if she could only shake the feeling that her time in captivity has dulled her own instincts, she might just be able to pull off one of the most dangerous—and wild—heists of her career.